# The Uncircumcised

## BY

## CHUKWUDI OKPALA

PublishAmerica
Baltimore

First printing

All characters appearing in this work are fictitious. Any resemblance to real persons, living or dead, is purely coincidental.

ISBN: 1-4241-4022-6
PUBLISHED BY PUBLISHAMERICA, LLLP
www.publishamerica.com
Baltimore

Printed in the United States of America

Amara and Dante
—the nectar of my life

It is too easy to forget Africa in America.

Alice Walker
*Possessing the Secret of Joy*


They have destroyed the things that hold us together,
and we have fallen apart.

Chinua Achebe
*Things Fall Apart*

The Uncircumcised

# BOOK 1

# Prologue

We have convened again this night in this beautiful hall of moons and stars, marked with voices of veteran storytellers, to tell a story, that is; not of gods; not of passionate love, the sort Chaucer told without telling you he copied; not of philosophic wisdom, but of human beings, of apollo, of dionysus, of athens, of thebes, of what you know, of how things fell apart when white man came, of what you may despise, spurn, and bleach out of your memory with the wand of time if you are not already charged with the current of the story, if you don't feel alienated from what you are, dull and rebaptized, born-again, seeking a haven where your past stands like a monolithic error, to be corrected, to be revamped like a soiled soul.

It is a story of men and women. I shall invoke many voices; If you see yourself in it do not let anger suffocate you. Strike your breast, dress in tattered clothes and walk in the public places singing sorrowful songs. And the sons of the soil shall be vexed at you. They shall wonder: they shall fight and they shall lose, because what holds them together has gone asunder, shattered like a pot of clay in the proximity of a huge stone. Hopeless. Death. Discord. They shall linger, eternally, like ghosts, for a concord, which they shall never find. Like blind men they shall grope in the dark, querying every object in their neighborhood, describing the elephant. Despair shall reign.

I shall not be scared of clichés, hyperbole, or any form of figures. I shall stir them into the pot of my story like culinary ingredient while baring several areas of human experience. You can object, but those who shall be charged with the current of this story shall be saved, salvaged; they shall be better and more human, like children of gods saved from the turmoil of sin and damnation.

My name is Angela. It was in my hometown. So I was told by my mother who was watching like the eyes of a god. The sun had just risen to the sky from his unknown home, basking with beauty. Trees freshened up with gentle gust. Their images stood by their roots, barely seen. Cocks crowed; birds chirped. Noises piled up: a man was tapping his palm wine; a boy chopping firewood, a loafer blowing his lungs out with a flute, inviting distant and ancestral spirits. There was our king. He was a worthy man in all respect; he's well-traveled, and he claimed that he had the answer to every problem contained in a book he stashed in his palace. No one challenged his authority or dreamed to challenge it. As such, he was approached with fear as a cauldron of tyranny. In that manner, he was little less than the Head of State or the President, whose autocracy was both numbing and draconian, was in destitute and in want of reason and intellect. Any phenomenon that he did not understand was faulty and should atrophy. His best wisdom showed when he met out undue punishment and decreed unjust laws. For that, people wondered how he came to power. Some thought of him as Gilgamesh. Yet nothing came from him, save hunger, starvation, and anarchy. Not every one saw that, though. Those who did not, saw him as the epitome of the human good spirit.

Like the King, he was old with bushy eyebrows and sagging skin; like the king, he walked wobbly as much as his thin legs allowed him. He tilted when he stood; and when he sat, he must rest his back. Like the king, he snooped and plugged his nose into other people's affairs, just because he found them interesting. Often times, he took charge of the affair and arrogated to himself the power to give life and death. Those who hated him did not speak ill of him in his face; they did so in his back, and, more so, in metaphors. Such fear gave birth to a series of songs:

*Do not touch the tail of a lion,*
*be it dead or alive;*
*for those who are afraid of me speak behind me;*
*when they shall see my face, they shall vanish.*

The humanity of the king, unlike the President, was rather more interesting, particularly for his erudition. He had a son whom he loved so much and had arranged for him to marry his friend's granddaughter. His name was Maduka, named after his father's friend. He read widely like a scholar and always inebriated himself with learning from east, west, north, and south. Nonetheless, he was simple and coy; twenty years old, and his greatest dream was to be famous. He was already famous for elegance, which everyone claimed that he had borrowed from some English book. He was always clean and cried when he saw a goat slaughtered, or a chicken's neck wrung. He carried himself well, though. He was worthy, too, not merely by his faculties, but the air spread by his father, stuffed with prestige and splendor. With flippancy he took his arranged bride because she was still in America. Little did he know of her, of how she looked or talked. Yet people fed into his flippancy, imagining the pedestal of the girl, how most worthy she must be. Her name was Tracy.

There was Elo, Maduka's youngest wife and only widower. She had a look of a woman that was sub-served, strained, harassed, and ruffled. From a distance, she's very beautiful, dark face, sizeable breast, plump hips that implicate a corpulent posterior. Verily when she talked, she's slow and calm; and scarcely did she rest; her hands were incessantly engaged in one thing or the other, building, destroying, rebuilding, and decorating. She was a good fellow, with rare wisdom that appeared only to resist challenges or to fit in—yet she was not bookish; she kept a good conscience as she prized her integrity above all things. She had only a daughter, Ifeoma, who was like her. For palm fruit does not fall away from its tree.

There was Anne, Nkem, Tracy, and Troy, who was only five then. They had just come back from America after Nkem's father died. And they came because Nkem's father had died. Nkem had apostrophized his name 'Kem and sweetened it with an 's' like a pot of podge-porridge to be served a hungry folk whose appetite admitted of something sizzling and confused only. His head was bald in the center and barricaded with fluffy walls of hairs that seemed to have been glued on. It was like an amphitheater, empty like his face on a head attached to his slender frame, tall and strong, with broad but not too wide a nose. He was a doctor, trained in America. In his entire world there was none like him to speak of medicine or surgery. He kept his patient in good condition with his magic. He knew the cause of all sicknesses, and he dispensed his art with an inimitable wisdom. He pursued all things that enhanced his practice and directed the flow of money to his pocket. He studied the bible very little, and very superfluous was his reckoning of it, because he loved money.

There was Ete, their servant.

One day Ifeoma and Tracy were in front of their compound, walled with barbed wire and populated with assorted houses, a duplex of Victorian architecture, joined unit by unit with huge pillars. It was magnificent. People journeyed from afar to see it as it was glamorous with its ever fresh landscape. They took the picture of it and toured its first floor that was filled with paintings of bizarre styles and furniture exquisite with their carpentry. But around this house was a low mud house with crumbling walls and a thatch roof. It was always dark in it, but very cool and soothing, very peaceful. It had no furniture save a dwarf chair by the kitchen fire. The rest was mud. Elo and her daughter, Ifeoma, lived there. She was fifteen, tender at heart, but she looked thirty for she was so mature and ruffled with domestic chores. She was a few years younger than Tracy. Her palms felt like coconut shell, her hair nappy and short and always shinning with oil.

"How do you do that?" Tracy asked Ifeoma who was weaving a basket.

"I jus do it like this," she replied and demonstrated, at the same time emphasizing herself because Tracy could not really understand her.

"What's that noise?" Tracy said, trembling.

"Noise!" Ifeoma said and listened.

"That's a woodpecker," she added.

"That's scary. In America you don't hear such noises from your house, unless if you go to the zoo," Tracy said and dabbled into the fashion that she identified with America, almost bringing Ifeoma to her knees with her description, seeking her inferiority, her worship with malaise and flippancy. But Ifeoma continued weaving her basket in lightness of heart.

"Let me try that!" Tracy suggested. She pulled her right hand to receive the thread, *ekweri*, that was made from palm fronds. Her hand was delicate, ripe like a fruit, whitish, soft and trimmed with nails polished with the color she had on her fat lips. Her long hair rested on her shoulder in dark array contrasting with her face. She was like a Barbie, more so when she opened her fat lips that house a shiny cluster of teeth.

"It is hard to do it," Ifeoma explained with piety.

"I can try," she proceeded.

"Ouch!" she screamed and dropped the *ekweri* which stuck in her finger and dislocated a piece.

"You don't do that. I told you it is hard," Ifeoma said. Tracy turned blue; her face shivered, and her whole body ached with a sort of pain, nameless, but excruciating with numbing paroxysm. She sulked and ran into the house. Not the mud house because she dreaded it like a dungeon, a cavern of worms and termite, but the other one, filled with grandeur.

"Mom! Mom!" she called. Her parents were chatting in the living room without benignity.

"Mom! You don't answer, damn it," she continued.

"What honey?" Anne came in flamboyance, as was her wont, shinning with costly apparels and cosmetics.

"I hurt myself."

"What were you doing?"

"I was trying to weave a basket."

"You don't do that. See what you get."

Kems stole a sarcastic smile only to plunge into a diatribe in his soul about fulfilling the King's desire to marry Tracy for his son. She is fragile, he thought.

"Tracy," he called. "You have to learn these things. We've come here to stay. Remember we have the task of living up to the king's expectation."

"She is beautiful enough. It is Maduka who is supposed to be pruning himself," Anne entered with an air of probity.

"No, it is Tracy. Maduka is son of the soil. He knows the ways. Tracy still has to learn."

"Learn?" Anne added and wondered, but her heart did not follow that wonderment. Her heart went with the feeling of being an in-law to the royalty and the pain of reducing her daughter to what she felt to be primitive and unruly. Nonetheless, she looked at Kems like a hungry panther. Kems rescinded into his shell like a turtle for her eyes became fiery. He was worried, and he wondered how he would get his family to adapt to the culture of their land. This was a huge thought on his mind, so huge that its weight pierced the bones of his head, which was writhing then with agony. He did not know what to do.

Nonetheless, Anne turned to Tracy and advised her to abstain from such retooling of objects, that it would destroy not only her nails but her fingers.

"You better listen now, unless you want to be like a village woman with leper fingers without nails."

As she was instructing her, Troy, her three years old brother woke from sleep. She did not hear his cry even as Tracy was trying to remind her.

"Mom, let me get Troy," Tracy said.

"Is he awake?" Anne replied.

"Yes."

"Ete! Ete!" She shouted.

17

"Madam, did you call?" Ete said in utter humility, dropping a broom by the door.

"Of course, I did. Didn't you hear Troy crying?"

Immediately, Ete rushed to pick up Troy.

Meanwhile, Troy's cry had gathered speed. His voice scattered everywhere. Elo came rushing from her house. When she came in, Anne and Tracy were talking while Ete was rocking Troy.

"Anne, Troy is crying," Elo observed with perplexity.

"Oh!" Anne said with sarcasm and took the baby from Ete and instructed him to get his food. At the same time, not letting Elo to go, she reprimanded her for letting her daughter teach Tracy how to weave a basket. Like a dove, Elo explained to her that her daughter might have meant well. However, Anne saw envy in her explanation. Then Elo left, shamefacedly. Almost. But there was agony more in her feelings because she could not understand Tracy's fragility.

"Ifeoma!" she called.

She came with a half-made basket in her hand, still weaving it. Her eyes were sodden, and she feared that she has done something wrong.

"What happened between you and Tracy?"

"She wanted to weave my basket. I told her no, but she took it. When she started, *ekweri* entered her finger. She don't know how to weave."

"You did not hit her?"

"No! As big as she is? No!" she said and sobbed.

She is agriculture, Elo thought; she felt satisfied that her daughter had not done something wrong.

The day dragged on, sizzling with heat. Crickets chirped with annoying combination of crescendo and rest. Elo walked rather unconsciously to the kitchen where she had kept some yam tubers for their afternoon meal.

"Peel those yams in the kitchen," she directed Ifeoma.

Without hesitation, Ifeoma went to the kitchen and began to peel the yam, singing songs, selecting the condiments for the taste of the meal they had decided to cook. Later, Elo entered with a heap of vegetable she had plucked from her garden, an assortment of green vegetables with flamboyant leaves, *ugboguru, ahi-haa, inine.* She laid them beside Ifeoma and began to pluck them off their tendrils and to slice them into smithereens.

"Make fire for me," she said. Ifeoma knelt down with her two hands on the ground—she looked like a sheep grazing. Her head was projected forward towards three big stone on which she placed a pot of water. She piled some dry leaves on the spaces between the stones, laid huge woods on them and blew forcefully to wake a dead fire. Slowly a faggot arose; followed by fire that began to leak the pot. By this time, Elo had finished slicing the vegetable, and with the dexterity of a food processor. She loaded the yam in the pot with tiny ounces of spices.

"Why do they do that? Is that how they cook?" Tracy observed from the window in one of the rooms in the house.

"They are cooking," Anne replied and stepped away from the window.

"I know. They don't have a cooker."

"They don't," she answered walking away and overtaken by boredom.

"Let's go to the king's house," she suggested.

"Is Maduka going to be there?"

"Perhaps! We are just going to get away. Ete!" she raised her voice. "We are going to the king's house if Kems asked you. Troy is in his room."

"No he is in the living room now, madam," Ete said.

She did not answer, but walked into her room. When she came

out, she had changed into a very tight pants that tailored her seductive body; her eyes was painted as her lips were, reddish like fire. Tracy was the same, but her hair flagged down her shoulder in abundance. She was in shorts, which showed her long tender legs, succulent and fresh.

Not long after they left, Troy began his usual cry. Again, it gathered momentum before Ete could pick him up. His face was bathed, as it was flooded with water that came from all cavities on it; his eyes were drab, mouth drooled, and his nose pierced with mucus. Interestingly, the mucus from his nose had linked with the one from his mouth; together, they traveled down his jaw like a chorus of termites. Ete attempted to pacify him, but he failed. Kems came and took him, wondering where his mother had gone. He cried further. Then Elo returned leaving Ifeoma to watch the food.

"Is he sick?" she asked and took him.

"No, he is just cranky," Kems replied.

"May be he is hungry. Where is his mother?" she asked.

"Ete, where is madam?" Kems said.

"She had gone to the king's house, so she said, sir."

"Oh! Our in-law," Elo added. "Find his food," she said and sang to him while playing with his face. Immediately, he calmed down and laughed. Kems left him with her and began to roam around the kitchen for his own food. Ete had not cooked because Anne did not instruct him to do so. Thus Kems encountered cold kitchen. His stomach boiled with hunger. He grew weary.

"Ete!" he called

"Sir," Ete answered.

"No food cooked?"

"Madam did not ask me to. She insisted that I follow her orders, sir."

Kems felt famished. Sorrow crawled in, tinged with perplexity, the sort that really numbed him, baring him of all powers of spirit, yet luring him vigorously to the confusion that was before him, the outlandishness of his wife. Ete was hungry, too, but he did not dare cook. As was his custom, he had scraped and eaten the leftover on the plate they used for dinner. Usually, he washed them after dinner. Not knowing what each tomorrow would provide, and since he did not believe in divine provision, he started leaving the plates. At times, he would joke that God actually put in his head the idea of leaving plates unwashed, so he could find some food in the morning when the pangs of hunger set it. He scraped them with the scrutiny of a detective, diving for the nugget of tasty crumbs.

Elo could not but overheard their conversation, though. She offered Elo a bowl of steaming vegetable yam. She took Troy with her, but little did they understand each other.

# 1

The sun had gone down; it was reddish on the horizon. Gentle breeze blew and silently made its way through the forest. Then it spoke, inviting the forest, with a whistling voice, shrilling all the same like a leper's jewelry. It made its way to the king's house. The same voice came, but tamed, with effluvium of a scent that arose from the blossoming flowers and fresh leaves. The house stood there, hidden like a lion, hoodwinking hunters as it preyed on them. No one saw it, but people knew that it was there.

"Where is the house?" Tracy asked on their arrival.

"It is there," Anne replied.

"Where?"

"There."

They disembarked from the car. A flood of eyes jammed them, gaping at their demeanor with relish, but from a distant of opposition. They were fresh, but the eyes were tawdry; they spoke English, but they spoke vernacular and stood in awe at their language; they drove, but they walked, and barefooted too, barbecuing their feet on the soil.

"Where is the king's house," Tracy shouted at one of them, a young man, whose stomach protruded so much that it seemed it did not like the rest of his body, that it wanted to go away. He said nothing, but rescinded to his group. Among them was a mendicant with a porous plate in his hand jangling for charity. His eyes were dirty, clothes threadbare, revealing his ashy skin and cicatrices of old wounds.

"Help!" he yelled, drawing back without being partial that they might be aliens, people from the sun or from the underground.

"I told you the house is there," Anne added, pointing at the avenue of shrubs with a fresh landscape and ignored the beggar, who hoped to participate in the good heart of the people who found time to visit the king.

"This is fascinating, mother. I did not know you can see a house like this here."

"Here it is."

They bypassed the mendicant and walked through the landscape in delicate steps, fearing that they might suffocate the grass. No birds chirped. Slowly a gate opened; the king and his wife stood there like sentinels with piles of smiles on their faces; more from his wife who stood there as a luster to his presence, the incandescence of his spirit, bulldozing through every sorrow that sought to inhabit his soul.

"That's Maduka's wife," the king said and adjusted his regalia, the elephant tusk and precious stone that hung around his neck.

"Why does she dress like that?" his wife asked.

"They have just come back from America," the king answered.

"America!"

Then, Maduka appeared and stood between his parents. He had only shorts on. His chest showed mounds of toned muscles and was lined with hairs that were the same size with those on his head.

"Your highness," Anne greeted.

You should genuflect, the king's wife thought.

"Welcome! I am not expecting you today. But you did well to come," the king said.

"You are always welcome," he continued. His wife's eyes became monstrous and began to turn green.

"This is Maduka."

"How are you?" Anne greeted.

"Fine, thank you."

"Maduka, you better go and put on your shirt," his mother suggested with austerity in her voice. Immediately, he dashed out of the room, which was then filled with camaraderie. Tracy combed through its beauty, imagining in her soul what happiness that's enjoyed by those who lived there. At the same time, her soul dwelt on living there, on walking side by side with the king. Her mother looked on, observing the movement of her soul as it appeared on her face through the arteries of joy and smile without abandoning the king with whom she engaged in a sweet conversation.

"I have been to many places, Europe, Asia, Middle East, but I have never been to America. I detest America, but I can't tell you why. What is like over there?"

"Mine is a lay opinion," Anne began. "It is okay, not the best place in the world, but good to live in."

"Better than here, I suppose."

"In a way, yes. Yet, it has its dark zones."

"Let me ask you to choose between America and out country, our home."

"The choice does not matter, because wherever I am I will have what I want."

"You are an intelligent woman, Anna…"

"Anne," she corrected.

"Anne."

They went into the parlor, whose décor struck a rhythm with the whole ambiance of the compound. Momentarily, Maduka's mother came in with a plate of garden fruits, *anara*, delicious green fruits she plucked from her garden. She took her seat beside the king.

"This is for you," she said and laid it on a wooden table. They partook of the fruits with relish and experienced a new taste, good and satisfying.

"This is exotic," Tracy observed.

At that juncture, Maduka's mother began to wonder; she took and ate one of the fruits, and it tasted the same to her as it tasted yesterday.

"You don't see this in America, do you?" she asked

"No," Anne replied. "But some of us bring it to America while returning, that is, if the custom officers allow them."

"You miss them, then," the king joined.

"Miss, no!"

Time passed by as they continued talking, rollicking in the moment, hoping to freeze it, to be there without any motion towards or from. Evening came, but it was still not dark. They rose to leave. Maduka's mother wrapped the remainder of the fruits for them and saw them off. Anne and Tracy were all words.

"Do you like what you saw?" Anne asked.

"Like? I love it," Tracy replied.

"You know if you are married to Maduka, who's the first son, you will be the first wife, and you will be in charge of all that."

"Supposing Maduka moves?"

"He shall not move. That's the custom. He shall stay to continue the lineage of his father."

"But he seems to be shy."

"He is, but he is a genius, quiet. You know what they say: geniuses are romantic and solitary. He might be shy now."

They kept silent suddenly and dangled through the rough road with a smooth drive into their house. Troy saw them while on Elo's bosom.

"Mom!" he shouted and rushed to her.

"Hi baby!" Anne picked him up.

"I was learning vernacular with aunt Elo," Troy said.

"You were."

"Kedu," he said with improper phonetics, letting his 'u' sound like 'ö'.

"O di mma," Anne replied, but she was furious. He set him down, and like a lion, pounced into the house. Kems was stretched out in the couch, blasé.

"Get up from there!" she yelled at him.

"What is it?"

"What is it?" she entered with fortissimo. "You left Troy to learn vernacular. Soon he will forget his English and grammar and spellings."

"But where were you? How much of that have you thought him?"

"That's not the question here. You left Troy with Elo."

"She is his aunt for god sake."

"To teach him vernacular?"

"Somebody will do that, if you don't. He's come to stay and English is not the language here."

"Not my child."

"Anne, listen. We are standing on the wrong feet here. We should not fuss about this."

"He hardly speaks English, and he is learning vernacular."

"He will learn. Remember English is not our tongue. We learned and even speak it better. Think of this: did you speak your language in America? If my mind is not deceiving me, I know very well you spoke English. You did not displace English with your language. Why do you want to displace your language here with English?"

"Only the poor speak it here," he said, and fiercely, she walked out of the room. Again, she picked up Troy without pampering him.

"You cannot speak that language now. It leads you nowhere. Believe me. It is impoverishing," she said.

"What's impoverishing, mom?" Troy said, staring at her. Anne began to laugh.

"It means that the language is bad," Tracy entered.

"But I like it; I like the way it sounds. I can speak two languages," Troy said.

"Oh! my boy! Learn another instead. Remember, you shall be going back to America someday, and they don't speak that language over there. Troy felt subdued, but his desire for that language was undaunted. He crawled down from her arms and rushed towards his father who had become very sorrowful, wondering what he had done wrong.

"Daddy, mummy said that I shouldn't learn our language."

Kems looked at him, tongue-tied, but his mind was filled with words of terror, lamentation, and sorrow. He looked at Troy for another minute and rubbed his head.

"Do as mummy said," he said.

"Why?"

"Mummy is right," he added, feeling the baseness and the irregularity of his answer. He felt it in his soul, in his blood, but his mouth betrayed it. Troy left, very dissatisfied; he sobbed his way to his room. His little experience with life was being shattered, and he knew it. But he had no resource for amendment; every biting time consumed him and left him hopeless, forlorn, and disgruntled. Then his soul grew larger with topsy-turvy. He became taciturn, thoughtful, and alone.

Meanwhile, Anne and Tracy were chattering, making belief about the future. Kems left the house, for it was not yet dark. His heart was heavy and his eyes were sodden with sorrow.

"Nkem," Elo called, "you came to our house. Is all well?"

"His face is dark. I don't think so," Ifeoma observed.

"Say that I'm well, but do I look well when my house is on fire. Do I look well when my son cannot speak my native language?"

"What are you saying," Elo asked with perplexity.

"You thought Troy some vernacular?"

"Yes, and he liked it."

'Well! His mother doesn't."

"Doesn't like it? What kind of a woman has she turned into? I remember when she was married first, before Papa sent her to you. She brightened every room, and people loved him. I cannot forget that! People were envious of you to have married such a nice girl. We cooked together in my kitchen. Here. Just for the fun of it, and she was my stronghold, for I was then scorned by my fellow women because I have not had a male child yet. Papa did not care! I did not care. Well! I cared, but I am not God. Anne use to tell me all these stories to cheer me up. What happened?"

"I beg you to tell me, Elo," Nkem began, resurrecting his past as an antidote to his confused spirit; as a recreation to soothe his battered faculties. It all started long ago. With a white man; you may not be privy to this part of the family. Everything was in peace before. You know that very well. In those days when we reveled the fruit of our labor, joined in a battle over a piece of land. We thought nothing of the way we talked, nor of the way we dressed. I dressed like a white man, though, I thought very little like him. He was insignificant. I despised him not because he was not human. He called whatever I did outrageous; our religion he called fetishism; our marriage he called buying and selling—little did I know of his which is worse than a commerce; it's a citadel of death, a propos of war and destruction. Some of them described it as such: "The ache of marriage."

*It is leviathan and we*
*In its belly*
*Looking for joy, some joy*
*Not to be known outside it*

We used to gather in free spirits and told stories, being innocent, young and harmless. You know. Oh! What a time past! a perfect past! An epic ingredient filled with heroes. We gathered without a sense of difference, without the pain of misunderstanding one another. We knew no difference for we were the same, one and all. Have you heard about how father welcomed him. 'Not because he is white,' he said. 'Because he is human and might have something that might displace some of our pains favorably. I believed him, even though I thought he was making a giant error.

One day he came, invited by my father. His name was Smith. His frame was slender, and his hair was flaxen. His face had red pulps, the ruin of mosquito assault. They bit me too, but I have never seen a pulp that red on my skin. He survived with what I called amity and openness, even though he was very talkative and imposing. Opposite him my father sat that day, relaxed like a lion that had eaten his full.

"What do you say, Maduka," he came in like a nightingale, travestying my father's name, "tomorrow we go to that portion of land. I want to send for my family, but before that I want to build a house, a home. Shall we do that?"

"Yes," my father replied. And from then onward, they were bosom friends. They unconsciously vowed never to harm each other, but to see one's goodness in another's. It is wearisome to remember. Father became a hero. He was revered because he welcomed a white man; he traded ideas with him. Next his family came. And they looked alike, a boy and a girl, with their mother whose frame was so flat that I wondered whether she was a plank. We looked at them in awe because they looked like angels; they acted like them, because we never saw their feet that were always housed in tall socks and leather shoes. They came to stay, and slowly they became human, exposing their feet, running around among us, getting dirty, getting injured, and putting sand on the face of their wound like iodine. Then, their drawl dropped; it thickened with their attempt to speak our tongue. They turned black and began to pass heavy mounds of foo-foo down their throats, and with ease too. Almost the same, but not quite; almost the same, but not African; disciplined and displaced, they were just mimic men,

Next, Smith took me to America to study medicine and as further extension of his friendship with my father. We were joyous. Only few people had gone there, and little did we know about them. I was happy, but I received my first linguistic baptism of error from Smith, for he butchered my name. You know; my father called me Nkemakonam. I do not remember what he called me. Each time a person called me, I got a new name. To avoid the butchery, I shortened my name to "Nkem," and he chose "Kems."

"What do you think America is, Elo? If you walk into America today will you know?"

"Yes, there will be white people everywhere."

"That's what I thought. But no. Wherever you see a white man, there is a black man, who might be in fear, in love, or indifferent where he is. It is like a hybrid corn, black corn matching after the white corn, perhaps not knowing that the other was there."

"They have black people there?"

"They do. They look like us,"

"Like us?"

"But they don't act like us. They are more American than African. Though, they don't believe it."

"How can you be African and American?" Ifeoma entered.

"I don't really know."

"They are legion. I lived among them. At first I was perturbed. I treated them with ignominy, for their dispositions were never short of insult and vituperation.

"Where are you from?"

"Africa."

"How is it over there? Do you have lion walking the street and shit?"

"Lions? I have never seen one until I came here."

Barbarism was all they knew about Africa, a wild theater where brutes gored their guts with reckless abandon. I weathered the storm and entered their society. Social responsibility. I did what they did. I spoke how they spoke.

"You aint shit."

"Were you at."

"You aint go' mess with my pips."

"I will burst you lips."

"You sucker."

"You motherfucker."

"It aint gonna happen."

I was just like one of them. I conked my hair; I made it look like a white man's hair. You should have seen me. But in my hand was the cement of my affair with Smith family. I was scared to bring it up for the fear that the blacks might call me a sellout, like they often did any of them mingling with a white man, threatening to kill him, especially with my conked hair.

"You white man lover."

"Jump into the slave truck; the auction has just started."

"Black ass nigger."

"Uncle Tom."

But, I always thought of how good and wonderful a white man could be. So when I saw more white men, even though I despised them, I always left a chance of loving them for they might just be bastardly colonials, like the Smiths. To my dismay, my story was shattered like a pot of clay, into smithereens with the force of reality.

One day! We had just finished a class, human anatomy. I was walking around the campus, which had predominantly white students. Smith's choice, of course. A choice I came to understand years later. But predominantly black school was nothing but a latrine, a ball-park for fratricide, invisible intellectual warfare, bag-biting. Yet, it flourished with black culture and vestiges of the talented tenth that appeared to demolish anything that attempted to overshadow it, either in body or spirit. Nonetheless, my school was huge with Byzantine and Greek architecture which I enjoyed and admired by slowly climbing the walls with my eyes until I became a bird, unaware of flight and height.

I was walking around with my classmates, Anita, Ashley, and Evans, the only three other black students in the school; so they told me; for I thought they were white from how they looked. They always carried their souls in a fragile crucible, blaming their mishaps on the school. I later found out that they came to the schools because their parents were alumni, because they were biracial and had trust funds. We spread our minds over the issue of human physiology.

"There is no spectacular difference between human beings and animals," Ashley said and span her head to remove the load of hair that was covering her face. Quite beautiful. Quite elegant. Quite European.

"The sizes are," I said meekly.

"Quite so, but that is a negligible difference. Size is not a characteristic. Speak of the essential parts, the function of the organs, the process of catabolism and metabolism."

"I do not agree," Evans came in. "Human beings, women to be specific, have vagina, the birth portal. Some animals use their anus for the same affair. Some even have to die."

"You are crazy," Anita and Ashley laughed.

"I know. But think! When we become doctors, that is what we shall be doing, examining human anatomy. A gynecologist digs his hands into the vagina of his patient; another will pick a man's testicles like bead, sizing them up; another will watch a woman deposit her baby."

"Deposit!" Ashley shouted.

"You are awful, Evans," Anita joined.

"I don't mean it like that. A surgeon cuts you open and sees what you will never see in your whole damn life. Medicine corrupts the sacredness of the human body"

"Shut up with your unrehearsed rhetoric," I said. "That's medicine without spirituality. Medicine restores the dignity of the human body. You are developing the mentality of doctors who think that they heal."

"Who heals Kems?" Evans wanted to know.

"You don't know?"

"Yes, who heals?" Ashley and Anita chorused.

"God, of course," I replied with eagerness.

"Get outta here!" They said together, and we laughed, though without rancor.

"You look so cute when you are serious," Ashley observed.

"Yes, he does with his chicken nose," Evans added.

I became mute, wondering why she had said that. At the same time, Anita, like a hawk, journeyed all over me. New sensibilities came over me, an alertness of who I was really, and how I really looked. For a moment, I was solipsistic until I saw before me, and in throng, cherubim and seraphim with cone heads.

"Do you have this type of church here?" I asked.

"What church?" Evan replied.

"Those."

"Church! They are no church. Those are KKK," he said and stopped. His heart beat accelerated, and he began to sweat profusely. At the same time, he shivered.

"What's KKK? They are cherubim and seraphim," I persisted, thinking that I was correct.

"You don't know. In a minute, these people will kill us, and nobody will know."

"What do you mean?" I said filled with fear; but they were very afraid to answer.

"What are they doing here if they are not cherubim and seraphim? I know them; that's how they dress in my town, preaching of the bliss in heaven."

Nobody paid me any attention.

"Let us see what they will do," I continued.

"That's social responsibility, isn't it?"

They dragged me out hurriedly through another way. Ashley held fast to me as Anita did Evans. Her pulse was very quick and jutted like she was in nightmare. I clasped my hand around her shoulder as I saw Evans did on Anita. Then she began like a popinjay, filled with words and wisdom, waiting to report to her master the result of her surveillance.

"I have never seen a man as crazy as you are. You call the Ku Klux Klan church people. Listen, they are known as haters, black haters, that is, killers of black people. For them, black is evil, or even nothing, something that should be blotted out of the face of the earth with any sort of tool. Their hatred has a long history; it goes back to the slavery time, the scourge of racism, when we were mere commodities. Little did people speak of us as humans, but as nigger. But we thrived, so to say."

"Nigger! Negro! It means black." I said banking on my auxiliary language.

"Yes, but the intention of the speaker distorts the meaning of the word. When they say nigger, it does not mean black; it means a worthless fellow. We kill them too, disparaged their power. Destroy this temple! We proclaimed. You know biting time is the springboard of heroes, of cowards too. We seceded and bore our own life, our own aesthetics, our glory, our little red book; we killed them, set them on fire: killing them kept us at peace. I am a nigger. Yeah! but get out of my face if your life is sweat to you. White man is evil; he is devil; he is a displaced black gene. That's the language. And the discord you see now is very old; it came with the beginning of time, with Adamic failure, with the banishment of Cain. Now it is a bramble tree, flourishing, ever green, ever agonizing. Believe me; what you see is microcosm of the evil that shall befall you here, this barbaric organization, America, that is controlled by avaricious and bloodthirsty thieves. They shall call you minority, reap the fruit of your labor and dominate you culturally. At times, I don't like thinking of it."

"I don't feel like that about white men," I said adjusting my hand around Ashley.

"You were not sold into slavery," they chimed simultaneously. I was nonplused for their tone of voice was stern and dastardly. I became scared thinking that I have missed an era in my life. I looked at them filled with pity and jealousy because I think that they knew what I did not.

"White man was in my country destroying everything we had," I said trying to belong, trying to fit into their experience." He ruled us, he thought us, but he's not extremely bad." But they rained on me like a punitive rain, devouring my senses, attempting to hate me.

"White man is essentially bad. He is not white if he is not bad," Evans said. "Look at me?" He said, his eyes became sharp like eagle's. I listened like a bird that had heard an alien song. I stood on one leg filled with wonder, but I bent my heart to them and told them the story of colonialism, the partition of Africa, the utter destruction of African culture, and how ready we *are* to forget that and live on. I don't remember now if we really forgot that.

"Slavery and colonialism are not the same. In one you have your soul; in the other, you have nothing," Evans said.

"No, I do not agree. There is lordship in both of them. There is a master," I replied.

"Listen to yourself. You cannot prove otherwise," he added.

"You have to understand that," Ashley began breaking free from my arms. "Slavery and colonialism are not the same. White man left you after colonialism; he left you in your land. In slavery he did not leave; he brought you into his land; he sold you the freedom he has defined, a sort of chain jangling around your ankle. You are half man; you are half animal; slavery is blotched to your skin."

"Tell him sis," Anita entered with enthusiasm.

"Who told you white man left after colonialism? Who told you that colonialism has ended."

"I Know; you have your governments."

"That's a facade, but it does not mean that I hate white man," I said with fear in my voice, which did not affect their union of hatred against white man, whom they willingly called the man. The Man! I thought of God, of a giant hero, of the man with both yam and knife confronting the throng of hungry and famished people, and only *thinking* of allocating his generosity according to his unchallenged discretion. But he stood there as a mean man, wicked and despicable. Yet, I did not understand, but we went on disappearing further from the sight of those costumed men, safe and happy. Then we laughed and cajoled ourselves, playing wild games.

Hush! I shall come in here. Autobiographers lie. It is always a disservice to let children be fed with lies. He is prone to lie now; he is hiding things now, making the story fit him perfectly, and forgetting the beauty of the story itself, the story as it is. I will bare the story with its scars and cicatrices, it's head and tail. No hyperbole. They played wild games, all right. It was then that Evans and Anita left, leaving him and Ashley who had begun to crawl around him with energy. They left for her apartment because she had a burning desire in her soul, which she believed would trigger friendship. Not long after they left, they entered a cozy room, elegantly decorated.

"Would you make love to me?" Ashley said. Immediately, Elo interjected and asked Ifeoma to leave. Ashley's attire flew as though it was possessed by her feelings. It glued to her body. Meanwhile, Nkem was outraged. As a matter of fact, he shivered terribly for he had never seen a woman spoke in that manner. Elo grimaced as though she did not believe him. But she smiled, wondering what it would be like to ask a man for love. She wondered so much because she had never done so and would not do so.

"What kind of woman is that?" she said all of a sudden, as though she had been hiding something. Nkem looked on. Nonetheless, Ashley went to her bathroom, fluffed her hair, brushed her teeth and washed her face.

"Do you want me now?" she said.

"Why would I?" he replied. She did not answer. She was hysterical, and she threatened him with hatred. What a fire to burn in a human soul! Her voice was a resonance of power, shattering and masculine.

"Get outta here!" she screamed.

"Why do I have to beg you to fuck me?"

He was outraged all the more. Her gentility had left her, and a certain type of animalism, an impropriety, which she vouchsafed as a rational action took its place. But she lay on her bed and cuddled, like a baby, tender and fragile and silent. Nkem left with ignominy, seeking to understand why she was so upfront, whether or not she was a harlot.

Later, he talked to Evans who was dissatisfied with his action.

"You are crazy, man. Are you gay? I have been dying to sleep with her since I met her. Don't you see how beautiful she is, and she likes you."

"Sleep with her! Is that all? Do you love?"

"She loves you, man, if not she would not ask you."

"Does she have to be upfront?"

"That's her scratch. She has to say so."

Nkem left, thinking he understood women, thinking of what he heard about uncircumcised women. But the following day, he went and apologized to her for his *inordinate* action. Yes inordinate! She forgave him and perched a kiss on his cheek. Nkem was exhilarated. He was joyous. They became very friendly now that he knew her need.

"Why are you telling this nasty story?" Elo asked.

"Wait, the real story is coming. Don't let your morality ruin it. It is coming and it has morale too; and it might explain my fear, my weakness, and why I'm distanced from my wife. Do you wonder why you would not act like Ashley? Is it your choice not to? Were you made not to?"

"A woman should respect herself," Elo observed.

"I believe that, just as a man should," Nkem added.

Another day and at different occasion, Ashley approached him with the same question. He yielded avoiding her chastisement. He was very perplexed, but happy. Later, again, he told Evans who had become the repertoire of his orgy with women. He patted him on the back. Then, he stopped thinking of white man; he thought of women, why they were so forward. He sought for his answer with indirection and opposition, through African women, Eugenia and Irene.

"Did they ask you?" Elo interdicted.

"No! They never, and they would not. I did. And whenever I

did they yielded actively; you could imagine that they were hoping that I would."

After one session with Eugenia, he asked her "would you ever ask a man to make love to you?"

"Not at all," Eugenia replied shielding her pride. "Are you out of your mind?"

"Why?" he inquired.

"It is not feminine to ask," she said.

"Is it masculine?"

"Of course! We have the choice of saying no."

"Really?"

He looked into her eyes and wondered whether she was telling the truth.

"A circumcised woman is a sexually silent woman," she began suddenly. "We are. We have lost the secret of joy, though we still enjoy it. We are never aggressive. We don't flaunt our desire."

"Circumcision did that?" he said.

"Circumcision is customary," Elo added.

"I believe so, but I do not know it does such damage," Nkem said.

"It does not," Elo replied with intrepidity

"Are you not half a woman then?" Nkem asked.

"No. You are half a woman without it."

They did not argue further, even though in his soul he resorted to believing that a woman should be circumcised to curb her of her aggression. He decided to believe that Ashley and Anita were not circumcised, fearing to confront them with it, or to make sure that their action was on account of it. He rehearsed the question in his soul.

Ashley, are you circumcised?

No. Why?

I am just curious.

Anita, are you circumcised?

No.

Are you circumcised?

No.

Many of them are not.

Nonetheless, the question did not bother him so much. Like a butterfly in the proximity of flowers, he perched from Ashley to Eugenia, oscillating between two contradictory personalities. Ashley became his girlfriend, and Eugenia his cousin.

# 2

Winter was fast approaching, then. The air, all of a sudden, got colder like ooze from a deep freezer. Trees bowed in homage and sacrificed their greenness. Some turned yellow; others turned red and fell to the ground in a lifeless heap; the trees slowly assumed unutterable nudity and apparent death. It was a divine regeneration: you have to die in order to live; yet, it was a real death for the birds that lost their love affair with flowers and trees and had to swallow the serenade they had rehearsed.

Nkem was not really used to that sort of weather. It was in their second year. Evans and Anita have drifted away from Ashley and Nkem—I shall tell you about them too. They only saw each other in class. Nkem had forgotten everything about white man. Little did he think of Africa and the Smiths; and when he thought of him, he saw him as a pretentious profiteer who used generosity as a facade of his evil machination, as any white man he had been told about. He was in love with a black woman, Ashley. He was able to stand with her amidst the flow of white women whom he had come to understand and whom he chose not to understand anymore. Amidst them, Ashley was ravishing, spectacular, and sumptuous, almost white. She was a magnet of animalism; her figure was a temptress itself. Not too many people survived it. Yet, she was in control, or so she thought.

On a certain day, the weather was nice, because it was not too cold. Almost everyone in the school yard dressed loosely; they bared their anatomy with abandon. Ashley, on her way to class, was dressed in a tight short that day with a sleeveless blouse. Her legs showed vigorously, and a swell of her breast inched out from the right corner of her blouse. Her hair flowingly hung on her shoulder and bounced in rhythm with her steps.

"Wow!" one man said and ran after her.

"Hi! Beautiful!"

Ashley stopped to talk to this man. He was muscular. His thorax was up to his neck. His head hung on his torso as though it was mechanically attached. She felt like a midget before him.

"Nice body," Ashley observed.

"Thank you! You are gorgeous yourself," the man replied.

"Thank you."

"What's your name?"

"Ashley. And you?"

"Pedro."

Silent stood among them for a while as they walked.

"Do you care for lunch?" Pedro asked.

"Can't you see? No. I am going to class."

"Class! What's your major?"

"Medicine."

"Wa-ow! Let me call you. We could catch a movie."

"I'll call you."

"Okay! I believe that I will see you again," he said and gave her his number and left, elated.

After class that day, Ashley came home hungry; she did not meander among her friends. She turned on her stereo and yanked herself on his couch. Not long afterwards, Nkem entered with a bag of fresh food.

"Hi! Darling!" she said.

"What's up?" Nkem asked.

"Nothing, Just hungry. Could you fix me something?"

"Yes indeed."

Nkem went to the kitchen while she lay on her couch. She flipped on the television. But the room had begun to steam with sweat aroma as a pot of onions sizzled on the stove, killing a piece of meat. Nkem was showing his culinary prowess as he adroitly flipped over the meat without spattering oil all over the range. In addition, he chopped some lettuce, cabbage, tomatoes, and onions, which he doused for a while in a bowl of vinegar. After, he arranged them on a flat plate, almost with a touch of art and beauty: a greenish base, red top and sprinkles of pink gathered from several sticks of carrot. On another plate, he placed the meat; then, like a waiter he took them to Ashley who had dozed off on the couch.

"Ashely!" he called.

"What?" she mumbled.

"Your food is ready."

Slowly, she rose. "You are so nice," she said having devoured the food with her eyes. She took a bite and commended Nkem.

"You are a good cook."

"I try." He was modest. He sipped a cup of water while Ashley ate silently.

"I can't let you go," she said after eating.

"I get it," Nkem took the plates away. And by the time he came back Ashley had gone into the bedroom.

"Ashley!" he called.

"I am here. Come on," she replied.

"I am getting ready to go. I have to meet somebody," he said advancing to the room.

"Who are you meeting?" There was violence in her voice as the tone was harsh and unfriendly.

"My cousin."

"Cousin! Well! That's okay," she was short and disappointed.

"Bye," she said and shut her door furiously.

Outside the door Nkem stood perplexed. He could not fathom what had overtaken her. But he left, a little dissatisfied and worried, more so for her manners than his well-being. Meanwhile, Ashley had come to the living room partaking of the program she left a while ago. Her face looked like a mound of feces forcefully dashed on the wall. There was agony on it; a trace of rejection stood there, and boredom, loneliness, and misery were parts of it. She flipped through the television, watching nothing in particular. Would that I get rid of him, he thought. This is not the first time. I always have to beg him. I have to see another man. Then she picked up the phone and called Anita.

By this time, the television was channel on 61 buzzing with picture.

"Hello."

"Anita."

"Yes! Ashley. What's up?"

"Not a thing really, but I gotta talk to you about this."

"What? Go on!"

"Nkem."

"Did he hit you?"

"No."

"I heard African men hit on their women."

"He did not. However, he is good and everything, but…"

"He is not giving it up?"

"Exactly."

"But you told me he is good."

"Yes, he buys me things, cooks for me, and washes my clothes, but…"

"I wish Evans could do all that."

"How is he?"

"He is okay."

"Does he satisfy you."

"Sexually?"

"Yes."

"He is a horse."

"That's what I need."

"But I don't like him like that. I'm gonna get another man, one who can care more about me."

"I'm thinking of the same thing, another man to compliment where Nkem fails."

"Yes, you can never get a man well suited. I gotta go. Evans is here."

"Who's that?" Evans asked with austerity, standing like a janitor at the hell's gate.

"Ashley."

"Is she okay? I hardly see her since she got serious with Nkem."

"She is just fine."

"Well! What are you doing today?" Evans continued. He finally sat down on a rough couch, thin at the edges, tattered and almost threadbare. It was too old, too; the only seat in the room.

In front of it was a coffee table, an oak, whose beauty was lost in dirtiness and age. Evans rested his feet on it and turned on the television set. It buzzed!

"I will have to rehearse my notes," Anita replied.

"Look at this?" Evans observed.

"What?"

There was a beauty pageant.

"Who cares about things like that, anyway," Anita observed.

"I do," replied Evans.

"And why?"

"It is entertaining," Evans responded while Anita mimicked him.

"I thought that's what you will say."

"Well!"

"Suit yourself. I do not care."

She distanced herself emotionally.

Ashley was still alone, bothered and lonely. She fished out her phone book and called Pedro. Pedro rejoiced for the call, but little did he know that he was at the end of a disturbed race, that he would be merely a pacifier, nothing real, nothing more. He jumped at the call beaming with joy, plenty of it. His heart became bogus with it, and a new feeling took over, a feeling of achievement and valor. He jumped into one of his nice clothes and left for her house. She received him, though not gracefully.

"You can leave now," she said a while later.

"Is it like that?" he yelled. He wanted something more. He wanted a relationship; he wanted to protect her, to buy her things, to cherish her, to call her his own. But all she wanted was what she got. Peace.

"Go now. I shall call you again," she added.

"Nothing that comes seems real," Pedro said.

"Oh yeah!"

"Yeah! Bitch!"

He was devastated. In another twist, he was happy; and he did not know the feeling that served his climate.

# 3

Winter picked up momentum in its devastation. No one was seen without being wrapped in bundles of clothes; ears and hands locked in gloves in the fashion of lepers. The air was still or even frozen, and everyone was fuming in the mouth like the exhaust of an immobile, running vehicle. The mouth was an aperture for releasing the cold.

It was evening when Nkem arrived at his cousin, that's Eugenia. It was still bright in the sky. Children ran around in the playground; some playing on the swing, going so high in the air with joy and excitement. Around them a child began to cry; a woman screamed at a girl who had mooned her friends. She approached her with agony, threatening to hit her.

"You are goin' to be a bad girl at this rate," she said. The girl cared very little and continued her game.

Nkem and Eugenia were watching through the window from an adjacent house. Their gaze made the scene seem silent, stable, unreal, and distant, for they said nothing. Suddenly, Eugenia stepped away from the window.

"Let me cook something for you," she said and walked into the kitchen. Nkem dragged himself to the couch in the center of the room, which was lavishly decorated; one painting there, a figurine here, a pot of flower there. He turned on the television like a master fatigued from a day's job, waiting on his mistress. Immediately, he was sandwiched between two uproarious worlds, the playground where the children had become vulgar and the world of the television where vulgarism stood out. He stopped and thought, very little though, about the meaning of what he felt, the automatic representation of the world in a television: voices clash for supremacy, yet without thought and eloquence, yet with bawdy and lewd innuendoes.

"Who do you think you are?"

"You aint shit, I say. And if you don't step, I'ma kick your ass."

"You aint got no ass, motherfucker."

"Fuck you man."

"Fuck you too. Fuck!"

"Change that channel," Eugenia screamed from the kitchen.

"Why?"

"You might start to talk like that."

"Eugenia, I have a language whose letters, whose phonetics, even phonology cannot support those words with a wand of meaning. One has to unmake me before I can speak like that."

"Really! I know Africans who do."

"They are unmade, that's what it is."

"Just be careful," she said and stirred some ingredient into her pot of soup. She turned it, and as she did, the whole room was covered with its aroma. Gently she put some on the center of her left palm and licked it. She smacked with satisfaction. She was happy, not just for the soup, but for Nkem, for whom she was cooking. She knew that. Then, she became tender, like a morning flower, shaken by the wind. Her voice lost volume; it became a sing-song like a bird's. She was inspired with desires, delights, a sort of energy, a little anxiety. She served Nkem who ate with concentration.

"Nice food, Eugenia." he said.

"I am a woman, now," she replied.

"Not all women cook."

"Well! That's true, but I would think all African women do."

"If that is the case, I give up," he said and shook his head. Darkness had not yet appeared in the sky. The voices in the playground slowly thinned away, giving way to the eerie voices of crickets and spiders. They were very audible. Eugenia and Nkem had gone silent, stealing glances from each other, climbing up and down imaginary mountains. Accidentally, their eyes met. They stood eyeball to eyeball. Armageddon set in Nkem's soul, a frightful co-existence of beings. He hamletized about sleeping with her. Unconsciously, he extended his hands toward her. She grabbed it saying nothing. As ancillary as that was, she yielded to a cross country with him. They ran far and wide; they crossed seven lands and seven rivers. And suddenly, he fell into a bottomless pit, where to live was not really nightmarish as it seemed from outside. And Eugenia did not care to pull him out or cry for some alien help; she left him there.

The following day, Nkem rushed off to school. Fortunately, he met Ashley on the school yard; they walked side by side. Her face was sullen. Her steps were inarticulate, dull like a bad story. Nonetheless, there was a chasm between them, adroitly sealed with silence; they were walking like two vertical walls on a journey towards eternity, never to link. She looked as though she had no eyes, no face. But on her face the sky was open, filled with grizzled sensation; in it, too, was agony, a perplexity that buried her hatred of what she loved.

"Speak to me Ashley!" Nkem pleaded. Ashley moved on silently and entered the classroom. With her entrance a new sensation filled the classroom and usurped the common recapitulation of sinful repast engaged by the students. Some listened as though they were before a cabal who had a knack for all eternal questions. Yet, she stirred in like a drop of black ink in a pot of white paint, spectacular, very visible, just like Evans and Anita, who were flanked by two white students, mimicking the cruelty of the creator in their aloofness and stoicism. They sat there, Evans and Anita, like specimen of color, lending visibility to blackness, far less than a leopard, a zebra. They were utterly visible. If no one saw them, there must have been darkness. But there was a risk in it, because, then, they will be nothing, but a voiceless phantom. However, Ashley sat. Her face was still sullen. Then, Nkem entered and sat behind Evans adding another drop in that pot of white paint.

"Is there something the matter between you and Ashley?" Evans asked, wondering about the gap between them in entering the class.

"Something? No," Nkem replied.

"She doesn't look happy to me."

"She seems."

"Did you say something bad to her?"

"No I just saw her on my way to school. Did she say something to you? Tell me now."

"No, but you know the heart of woman by the impression on her face."

"What impression! She is laughing over there."

Evans looked. She was talking to another classmate, Madison, a man who was telling her a joke. He was sententious like a parrot. His voice was distancing as he accentuated every bit of his metaphor that hovered before him in place of real concepts. He gathered his characters, and vigorously bared his device, threading where multitude feared to go. They were not mere aggregates composed of traits, but an organic person filled with attention. He contemplated. Ashley was mute, admiring the movement of his lips. She looked as though she did not breathe with her hands folded on her chest. She listened with her eyes, ogling every bit of his aspects, his mouth that was perpendicular to his chin. She was immobile, almost obliterated. In her soul, however, was a feeling, a feeling of love, which kept multiplying, which became a bore, then love again. She wanted Madison; she wanted to crush him on her chest, to ease the ache that was there: it was like fire. And the thought that she wanted him like a woman left no shame on her face. Rather, it bred a hatred for Nkem. He hated Nkem as she believed that he was destroying her naturalness, her spontaneity as a woman, her secret of joy. Again, it bred intimacy, which grew out from her soul towards Madison like a tree branch in tropism, without convulsion or torture. But from his mouth so many thing came forth, even a caricature.

"I am telling you a story of two people, Apollo and Dionysus, two utterly different people, who, however, could not live without one another. In the absence of one the other turns into a brittle carcass, waiting to shatter, lonely and evil. Apollo is a calm man, beautiful, quiet, divine, with unshakeable faith in his principles. Dionysus is nothing in proximity to this. The most intimate analogy that would bring his character close is that of drunkenness, extremism, debauchery, narcotic drought, and madness. In him nature is enthroned, everything is permitted.

Yet, Apollo could not live without him; he always wanted a spice of barbarism just as Dionysus wanted the cushion of moderation and gentility. Thus, they looked at each other sexually, two men, but Dionysus prevailed and checked and destroyed Apollo. Consequently, Apollo lost his voice, his place, and kingdom…"

"Wow! Wow!" Ashley mechanically said.

"It is a true story, and written in every heart," Madison added, adjusting himself. "But let me finish."

"What are you doing after class?" she asked, pretending not to have heard him. Her face beamed with light. She wanted to embrace him.

"Nothing," he replied.

"Can you come to my house?"

"Of course! What time?"

"An hour after class," she replied loading all her effort towards damaging Nkem emotionally, to discontent him peevishly.

"That means that I have to rush home."

"You don't have to."

"By the way, is something going on?"

She could not answer before the professor entered. Silence entered with him and slowly ate all noises like a monster. He dropped his books on the lectern and removed his glasses. His face shone with enthusiasm, as his eyes were animate with a physician's sensibility; they stood on his face, sharp like eagle's; his moustache extended over his mouth. His hands were firm and beautiful, aristocratic. There was no doctor in the school like him. He knew medicine; he knew the cause of every sickness; his words were apothecaries, and he was ever ready to cure any disease, at night, in the morning, or afternoon.

"Now, future physicians!" he began in a hoarse voice. "Ethics is our subject. What is it?" Those students who remembered the content of the previous class volunteered their rehearsed opinions, cited Aristotle, Mill, Bentham, and Kant, though not profusely and not with conviction.

"What exactly did Kant say?" the professor asked more directly.

"Yes! Categorical Imperative. What about it?"

"Act only on universalizable principle."

"Yes."

"Treat human beings as ends, not means to an end."

"True! But is that possible? Is there a moment in our lives we do not infringe on that principle?"

"How ethical then is a principle that is impossible to live by?" a student asked.

"Its impossibility, as such, is what makes it ethical. Ethics demands our perfection, or our striving for perfection. Such a principle is critical in our profession, and, as such, should be the blood in your vein. Do not let your ego make a judgment for you because somebody might die. How would you feel if you are to be blamed for the death of another man? How would you feel if you are responsible for the life of another man? I shall tell you the feelings are not the same. One is like the night, filled with darkness; the other is like the dawn, the disappearing act of the evil one, a new sensation, filled with joy, godlike. A good doctor heals, he creates, he suffers, all for the goodness of men; a good doctor lives by moral principles...."

"I think ethics mocks our imperfection. We are prone to error," a student observed.

"Exactly! But the distinction between two people lies in their behaviors and intellects, which exude their moral principles."

"Which principle should be our guide since they are all contradictory?"

The bell chimed. Noises came back, arising from the feet of the students; they shuffled through and through the room. The professor gathered his books and left.

The buzzword then was ethics! Are physicians subject to morality? Who is really a good physician? When is it proper to let a patient die? The professor planted a seed of wonder in their souls.

"What are we going to do Nkem? Let's grab some lunch," Evans suggested among a pocket of few students who were still bemused by the ethical questions.

"No, I have to see Ashley," he replied.

Immediately, he left and rushed to Ashley's, thinking of meeting her on the way. He did not. He knocked on her door.

"Welcome Madison," she said behind the door.

"No, it is Nkem." Nkem entered, flushed with emotion. He dropped his book bag like a cross. His mind battled a fiery sensation. He stooped to pick up his bag up again. He could not. Instead, he slumped on the couch and looked intently at Ashley, trying to see and understand. Her hair was all over her face in curls. Looking back at him, she jerked her head to remove the hairs that was clouding her face; her face was naked, but he knew that he should not try to kiss her.

"How are you?" he said.

"Just fine," she replied without interest.

"Is anything wrong?"

Ashley hesitated. Her hatred for him crept back into her soul. She walked around the room like hyena, aimlessly and frustrated.

"You are beautiful," he said. Ashley smiled and looked at her watch.

"You have told me that before," she replied.

"Have I?"

"Would you worry if I go with somebody else?" she added.

"Somebody?" Nkem said with skepticism. "Yes. You know I would."

"Why would you? You don't love me."

"Love you! Goodness! I love you!"

"You don't make love to me. I would rather we remain as friends now."

Nkem upturned his face to the ceiling. There was darkness everywhere. But there was a spark of light that made him fret with certain consciousness, a rejection, and an impropriety. 'Recklessness is a woman's revenge on man always,' he thought. 'Sex, circumcision,' he thought too. "Is it really true?" he wondered and measured Ashley's dispositions against Eugenia. He was not satisfied.

"Are you my friend?" he asked.

"Yes."

"What does that mean?

"That you can come here and talk to me; things like that."

"What have I been doing before?"

"I don't know."

"When the sun goes down, Ashley, when the moon comes up in the sky, darkness begets a face, a face that stares at one through one's window."

"You know poetry, I know."

"If I do, it does not pay to recite it in the market place. And know that I do not hate you." He grabbed his bag and left.

Behind him Madison came with an anthology of roses. Some incurved, some wide spread, with a sparkling redness. He did not know why he was asked to come, but he thought that flowers would speak very well of him.

"This is for you."

"Thank you. That's nice of you." She smelt them and perched a kiss on his cheek.

"Do you like it?"

"I love it," she said and kissed him again. Then she arranged the anthology in a vase and set it on her coffee table.

"This is beautiful," she said again filled with smiles. She was full of joy; her dream was coming true. She jerked her head, then, the difference came. Her eyes were bathed in tears. Her mouth became sensual and watery. Her body was stiff with a peculiar emotion, as though she was ready to kill whoever disapproved of what she was thinking.

"Here I am," Madison said. "What's the big news?"

"There is no big news. I just want to see you."

"Here I am."

"Finish up your story about Apollo and Dionysus."

"You like it."

"You could tell me another one."

"What's there to tell? I'm not really a storyteller. I only tell what I heard other people tell, I appropriate them and make them mine."

"Yet, they are your stories. Tell me one."

"One! Okay! This I heard long ago. I shall tell it as I heard."

"Go on," she said, looking into his eyes without shaking.

"There was a rich man in the city of Gafsa," he began. "Among his children was a pretty girl with charming manner. Her name was Alibek. She was not a Christian as one would think coming from that city, and was not yet circumcised as was required. She had heard many of her neighbors spoke of their Christian faith, the service to God, the punishment in hell, and the damnation of the sinners. One day she asked one of them, a man, how this service to God was performed. He told her that the

THE UNCIRCUMCISED

people who serve God best were those that avoided the worldly and temporal things. So Alibek, who was very young and naïve, did not tell anybody her discovery, to see whether it was true or not. But she slipped away the following day in the direction of the mountain oasis of Mides, motivated by a childish enthusiasm rather than by any well-considered inclination. It was an exhausting journey; but buoyed up by her enthusiasm, she reached those lonely parts a few days later. Seeing a hut in the distance, she turned her way towards it because she was famished. In the hut, she found a holy man standing at the door; the holy man was surprised to find her there and consequently asked her, 'what are you looking for little one?' 'God had inspired me to enter your service,' she replied.

"Seeing how young and naive she was, the holy man was afraid that the devil will ensnare him, should he keep her. Thus he said to her: 'My daughter, not far from here there is a holy man who'll instruct you far better than I can in the thing you are seeking for. Go to him.' He sent her away. She went to him, but he, all the same, sent her away. In this manner, she continued until she reached the cell of a young hermit called Rustico, who was as good and pious as he could be, and she made the same request of him as she had done of the others. Now, he, anxious to put himself to test, did not send her away or pass her on as the others had done. Instead, he kept her in his cell. And when night came, he prepared for her a bed made of palm-fronds in one corner and told her to lie down.

"When this was done, it took no time at all for his resistance to come under attack from temptation, which easily got the upper hand, so he turned tail after rather a few assaults and conceded victory. He piled on one side all pious thoughts and devotions and holy disciplines. He indulged himself in dwelling upon her youth and beauty, and in considering ways and means to persuade her towards his goal without leaving her to think that he was a dissolute man. First, he tentatively questioned her and established that she had no previous carnal knowledge of men and was every whit as simple as she appeared to be. Second, he verified her natural disposition to carnal pleasure, then he devoted many words to explaining to her what an enemy of God, the devil, was; then he made her understand that the service the Good Lord found most pleasing was to put the devil back into hell, to which the Good Lord had condemned him.

"'How would this be done?' the girl asked.

"'You'll know in a moment,' Rustico replied.

"'Just watch what I do and copy me.' He stripped off his clothes; the girl did likewise. Then he knelt down as if to pray; he made her kneel facing him. In this posture, as Rustico appetite grew at the sight of such a beauty; he saw that she was not circumcised; he experienced the resurrection of the flesh, and Alibek looked on in amazement.

"'Rustico,' she shouted. 'What's that thing you have got there sticking out that way? I don't have one.'

"'Oh my daughter,' Rustico said. 'This is the devil I've been telling you about. Look, he's making such a nuisance of himself. I can hardly bear it.'

"'Well! God be praised!' cried the girl. 'I see that I'm better off than you, for I don't have the devil.'

"'You are right. But you have something else I don't have.'

"'Oh! what?'

"'What you have is hell. Mark my word, I do believe that God has sent you here for the salvation of my soul: if this devil goes on molesting me and if you are willing to show me this much mercy, you'll let me put him back into hell. This way you'll give me the most enormous comfort and do God the greatest and most welcome service, if you really have come to these parts to serve Him, as you say you have.'

"'Oh! my father', she said. 'Since I've got the hell, let it be just as you wish.'

"'Well! God bless you my daughter! Let's go and put him back into hell so he'll leave me in peace,'

"This said, he laid Alibek down on one of their beds and taught her the right posture in order to imprison that creature accursed of God. And the girl who had never yet put any devil into hell found it a little painful the first time, and said to Rustico: 'What a horrid thing this devil must be, father! What a real enemy of God, for when he is put back inside, he hurts the very hell itself and not just other people.'

"'It wont always feel that way', Rustico said. And just to make sure, they put him back six times before they got up from the bed, and left him for the moment so deflated he was quite willing to subside. But as the devil raised his head many a time thereafter, Alibek was always there at his cell, ready to deflate him; she started to acquire a taste for the exercise and would say to Rustico: 'I can see how right they were, those good men at Gafsa who kept telling me what a pleasure it was to serve the Lord. I'm sure I can't remember ever doing anything I found so enjoyable as putting the devil back into hell. So it seems to me, anyone who bothers about anything else than serving the Lord is an ass. Henceforth, she went the whole time to Rustico saying: 'I have to come serve the Lord. Let's go and put the devil into hell.' And she would remark as the devil was in the hell, 'why does the devil eventually escape the hell? If he stays in it as long as hell welcomes him and keeps hold of him, he'd simply never leave.'

"So Alibek kept after Rustico, urging him to the service of the

Lord until she had worn him threadbare, and left him feeling chilly when he should have been at boiling point; he was dying without energy. He explained to her, then, that the devil was to be punished and put back into hell only when he got above himself. But noticing that Rustico was no longer inviting her to help put the devil back into hell, she said to him: 'Your devil may be whipped and giving you no more trouble, but my hell is giving me no peace at all. So the least you can do is let your devil soothe the itch in my hell, just as I helped you take your devil down a peg with my hell.' Rustico looked at her, a little furious, yet inarticulate. He said, 'there is death in that if the devil does not take time; it shall deflate never to rise again.' With these words there was a kind of truce. Yet, Rustico's devil and Alibek's hell remained at loggerheads owing to the voracity of one and limpness of the other; yet, Alibek's desire was unquenchable, and people who heard the story have said that it was because she was not circumcised; but it so happened that fire ravaged Gafsa, and Alibek's father was burnt to death in his house, together with the entire household. Consequently, Alibek inherited all that he possessed, whereupon a young man called Neherbal, who had squandered his own fortune in high living, set out in search of her. When he found her, he took her to secure her father's estate before it passed over to the Crown, owing to intestacy, much to Rustico's relief and to her immense reluctance. Neherbal became the joint inheritor of the family fortune. But she was questioned by the womenfolk as to how she had served God in the desert— this was before Neherbal had taken her to bed—she told them that her service consisted in putting the devil back into hell, and that Neherbal had done wrong in taking her away from such service.

"'How,' the women asked, 'is the devil put back into hell?'

"The girl explained how, with the aid of words and gestures, and she provoked them to such a gale of laughter; they haven't stopped yet.

"'Don't be upset', they told her, 'my child we do it here too, and Neherbal will serve the Lord with you perfectly well.'

"Then the women passed the word round the city until it became a proverb that the most agreeable service one could render to God was to put the devil back into hell. This proverb has crossed many waters and remains current here too with us as you know."

"What happened to the hermit?" Ashley inquired

"He remained in the service of the Lord, to my knowledge."

"That's really interesting; are the people suggesting that she enjoyed what she did because she was not circumcised? I cannot really understand that."

"That is what they said according to the story. Whether it is true or not, I do not know."

Ashley, then, suspended judgment, not knowing whether or not she was privy to the essence of feminine being; not knowing whether or not what she felt about sex was common among woman, especially since she was not circumcised and did not know any one who was.

"Let us put the devil back into hell," Ashley said anyway and advanced to Madison, kissing him, and not pretending at all, doing what she considered natural to her.

"No," he shouted.

"Come on!"

The hell caught fire while the devil entered only to come out in fear and trembling, yet a devil.

# 4

It was not evening, yet. The weather was a bit windy; not bad at all. Sun was shinning too. The mixture produced an interesting atmosphere; throngs of students wandered about seemingly aimlessly, only to bask in the good weather, to cajole winter. Winter! Where are your pangs? They thought. Or so they seemed.

Anita and Evans met with Nkem on their way from the restaurant. They were full, energetic. Nkem was a little forlorn, though his face was calm and clean; his eyes clear; but his voice was scratched with pain and rancor.

"Did you see Ashley?" Evans asked.

"Yes," Nkem replied.

"What's up with her?"

"We are now friends, she said."

"She dumped you?"

"That's what it is, but I think she like the euphemism better."

"What did you do?"

Then he began to tell his entire story filled with pity.

"Well, I shall smack her face," Anita interdicted, "even though she seems to know what she wants."

"Some times women don't," Evans added.

"Hei!" Anita contested.

"Don't take it personal, there are plenty of women out there," Evans suggested.

"Is that your answer?" Nkem asked, a little furious.

"But it is not your fault; you have to understand that," Anita explained, trying to show her how a woman takes a broken heart. Suddenly, Nkem dabbled into laughter. His whole body shook. He became a spectacle, as he was loud and wild. He laughed further as though laughter reinforced his pride. His laughter was euphoric; it exalted him; then he thought he would love Eugenia, a new specimen, who could be caring, who's African. Then, he tried hard to scorn Ashley, to hate her, but he could not see in her anything wrong, something odious, save her pretty face, her numbing beauty. He became weak.

"Are you going mad, Nkem?" Evans asked, perplexed.

"Madness does not have my name. I am only stupid, and I'm going home." He left, but went to Eugenia.

* * *

A month came and passed. Nkem was not again totally dissatisfied with himself. When he felt that he's hurt, he thought of Eugenia who entered his soul like an angel of light, radiating all crevices with love, mingling with all his emotions. Yet, Eugenia did not believe that he would come closer to her as she had come to him, because she thought he had more interest in American women; she doubted her feelings, but she loved him all the same.

At the same time, Ashley had stopped seeing anyone, though

not out of choice. She was completely starved, and the next option for her was harlotry, which she spurned so much. She felt a stone in her soul and thought of his future as a sorrowful mystery. At this time, she was nauseous and dizzy. She could not imagine herself being happy any longer as she was filled with nausea. With her last energy she picked the phone.

"Anita, please, I am sick; help me," she said. Anita rushed immediately to help her. By the time Anita came, she was lying on the floor, writhing with pain; her eyes were turned in their sockets. They were white, as the black iris had gone faraway; she looked scary, like a monster, something ghoulish, and moonlighting on a Halloween street.

"Ashley! Ashley" Anita cried. She did not answer.

"Ashley!" she cried again and dial the emergency number. Then, she checked her pulse. They were okay, but her body was cold and rigid.

"Ashley," she called.

"Anita," Ashley slowly began in a voice filled with anguish. "I feel awful."

"You'll be all right. You'll be all right."

Then the paramedics came and saw Anita standing by her with a stethoscope.

"What's the problem?" one of them rushed in.

"I can't tell for sure."

The paramedic paid her no further attention and began to resuscitate Ashley. He opened her mouth and flashed a light into it. He opened her eyes and did the same. Next, he checked the color of her fingernails.

"Are you a relative?"

"She is just my friend."

"We have to take her to the hospital," he said.

"That's okay."

"Would you sign here?"

Anita hesitated for a reason she could not put her fingers on. She stood there looking like one craving an alien wisdom, a wisdom that has the eloquence of turning her into a god. Yet, on the corners of her eyes were perplexity and wonder, spectacular like a diamond in a dark crucible; like a spark. She was silent while they put Ashley on a stretcher and into the ambulance.

The professor was on duty at the hospital. He was in a blue overcoat with a blue head wrapper. His moustache stuck out abundantly.

"Ashley," he shouted at her. But she did not answer. She was mute; her eyes had turned again. In haste, he gave her antibiotic injection, fixed her onto oxygen. He drew some blood as he had become fearful for what the ailment might be. Ashley did not talk; she did not bathe her eyes; she was dead; yet she was alive. Meanwhile, Anita was standing in the lobby patiently, but desperately, waiting to hear what was wrong with her. "Acute pneumonia," the professor reported. His heart dropped on account of what she felt. In silence, he left and performed further test for HIV. By this time, Ashley had been revived. She could not talk, however. She was feverish, very tired, and hungry; yet she could not eat what was set before her.

Next, she was taken to the north ward, a section for those destined to die. And that was the only place she could stay.

"It isn't cancer? It isn't cancer? Is it?" Anita asked a nurse who was wheeling Ashley to the ward.

"Of course not," the nurse answered nonchalantly, wheeling her into the ward. A terrible sight! An unforeseen destruction of men by a disease they named. They entered, and she was welcomed by a throng of famished people with drips wired to their arms. They lay their weak, with bulbous stomach, stiff and never ready to burst, with skinny bones that will not break, with withered skin that will not rot, enveloped in pain with the proximity of death, annihilation, perhaps.

"Nurse! Nurse!" one called.

"Yes!" one came quickly and administered to his needs fearing that he might die anytime. Anita watched; she stood by Ashley, consoling her, reminding her doctors save life, how she shall go home and become a doctor. Then, the professor came.

"Excuse me, Anita," he said.

"Is she going to stay?" Anita asked.

The professor did not reply. Rather, he directed her attention to Ashley who barely talked.

"After the analysis," he began in a quarrelling tone, agonizing in his own words, "we found that you have HIV. It has developed tremendously. There is no guarantee that it will not turn into AIDS tomorrow; however, I have prescribed some medications to fight it."

Consequently, Anita broke into tears and left the room. Ashley was, however, calm. In her mind were men pushing devils into hell.

"It's over now," she said.

"We shall keep you here to monitor you," the professor said and left.

Then Ashley was hunted by fear. Men flew away from her soul: death winged in like a little thought, fertilized with fear and desolation. She felt that the door to life had been slammed on her face. Everything was unpleasant, and she had to look at her roommate whose stomach was bulging under her white sheets, whose head was invisible, who's mute, her equal now. From time to time, she screwed her face, itching for something to hear.

Then, the uncultured noises and the breath of a dying spirit would come, weary. She would have loved to tell her to stop, but she was not in charge.

Evening came. She was lonely. She remembered her friends. Nkem stood out like a star. She remembered her poetry, "when the sun goes down, when the moon appears in the sky, darkness begets a face." She looked at the window. There's a face on it looking at her. She cried, because it was her face.

* * *

The moon did not wait for anyone; it was December. School continued as though nothing had really happened, although many students were perturbed about Christmas and going home. They still enjoyed themselves in mixed feelings, coupling sadness and sorrow. Ashley was still in the hospital, quarantined as her AIDS had blossomed. Whoever came to her wore metal armor like medieval knights. Death stood on her face, which was no longer a face, but bones covered with flesh. Her eyes were poppy. Her cheek was in her skull. Her breast had disappeared, as her legs had become drumsticks. Yet, she was human, but not more than vegetable.

The weather was calm that day, not like the usual December weather, when Nkem came to see her having received the news from Anita. He came with a bouquet of flowers and a basket of fruit. He had no metal armor. He had just finished fighting with Eugenia who threatened to quit him if he would visit Ashley in the hospital.

"You are going there, Nkem," Eugenia began like a bell tolling away a life span

"Yes, I am. But I will be back," Nkem replied.

"Back where? Don't you know what her disease is? AIDS! It is contagious, and it kills. I don't want you to bring it back here," she was furious.

"It is only transmitted through bodily fluids. You don't get infected when you care for or visit an infected person. She is still human," Nkem added, a little defiant.

"Go and trade your idealism somewhere else."

"Idealism? Is that what it is when you recognize the humanity of another person?"

"That is what it is when you cannot see the danger in your action. You are killing yourself."

"Let me give you a hypothetical. Let us say that you are sick, and that you are diagnosed with a deadly disease, so terminal that you will die. I was told about it, but I did nothing. I disappeared. How would you feel?"

"If I have expected you to care, I would be devastated."

"If not?"

"Nothing."

"But if I still cared despite your lack of expectation? Is my act desirable in itself, or is it so because you expected it?"

Eugenia became silent examining her answer in her head. But she did not say it for she knew about its impropriety, its cruelty and wickedness. "This is different," she said suddenly. "She has AIDS, a sexually transmitted disease. It means that she's loose, promiscuous. That's the point I'm making."

"She is human, too."

"Just don't come if you go."

Nkem did not want to imprison himself in her fear like Anita and Evans had done on their fears. They had disappeared.

That day, he came and sat beside Ashley and told her stories of life, the frailty of man, the beauty of the dead.

"The world is a theater, Ashley," he said, "and each and every one of us performs a drama that ends with our death and disappearance. Absence. Is it absurd? No! Is it understandable? May be! And it depends! It is just unfortunate, but we surmount with love. There is no sorrow in a heart that loves—there is no death there. It only transforms."

"You are a wonderful person, Nkem. It is a shame I'm seeing it in my dying bed," Ashley uttered her first few meaningful words since she was brought to the hospital, and slowly too, but without pain.

"You are a wonderful person too."

Later that day, he arrived at Eugenia's flushed with emotion. His face was blank, and he sweated around the rims of his hair. The following day Ashley died. No one remembered her afterwards.

# 5

Elo was there taciturn, twisting her hands in amazement. But I shall stop now. I have finished the excellent parts of the story; I shall let him to continue his story now for no lies can be told now. All there is to tell now is for his honor. It is not my part to tell a tale of honor of whom that has mouth and power to do so. Tell your tale if you are honored in it. But do not if you are not, for you might tell a lie to save your face.

It is a long story Elo; I was finishing my studies. I moved away from everybody, from Eugenia too. I became lonely, flirting with despair and boredom. My spirit became devilish and bothered me with diabolic feeling; lewd and bawdy affairs appeared enticing to me. I cherished them, though I hesitated to accept them. Then I sent words back home to my father that he may look for a wife for me. That's what most people were doing. I could not marry Eugenia, even though I wanted. She changed, lacking in human compassion. Then I married Anne whom my father had chosen as you know. The fever of irritation! I shall tell you now what ails me, how things melt into agony. I won't tell you a lie; she was beautiful, well built like an angel. She satisfied my desire for a beautiful woman. She had a quivering smile which overtook her whole body. We acted freely and held no one responsible.

"But we don't eat beauty," Elo joined.

I know now. Then, it was as though I was in heaven. She cooked for me; my food waited on the table for me when I came back from work. My house was cleaned; my clothes were cleaned too. I never saw her idle. She was either sorting one thing or the other, sowing a cloth.

"How are you, Anne?" I asked her one day.

"I am fine," she replied.

"You like America?"

"Yes, but it seems very boring. I don't know anybody. Sometimes, I feel as if I am dumb while you were gone."

"Oh no! I shall take you to this party this coming Saturday. You shall meet some people."

That Saturday came. The weather had not been nicer than it was. The sun was full bloom, very bright and clear with a gentle breeze that was soothing. It was beautiful. And Anne was beautiful too, ravishing. Her face was meek with lashes of well-chosen cosmetics, and her attire was novel and spectacular.

We came to the party; it was theatrical, legion, a panoply of styles, varied mannerism. The few people I knew were filled with probity as their wives tagged along them. One of them, Ojukwu, came along—he was still a bachelor, though; but you cannot tell for he was getting old and seemed to have married long time ago. He was dressed in *babariga*, and his eyes were darting here and there with atavistic yoke, trained to see only difference and anomie, trained to see colonialism even in its embryo. Once ago, he had confronted a white man, to my chagrin, who preached to him of the universal brotherhood and advised him of the evils of slavery. 'The sins of the fathers are always visited on their children. Or as we say in our place, when one finger drips with oil, others shall drip too,' Ojukwu responded to him in defiance.

He saw me that day, and was filled with joy; he shouted my name.

"Nkem!"

"Ojukwu, you are here. Meet my wife," I said with some air of integrity. Ojukwu's eyes dilated with admiration while he stared at Anne.

"How are you?" he said.

"Fine," I replied and passed him by.

"Nkem," Emma greeted.

"Emma, how are you? Where is your wife?"

"She's over there with her sister."

"Call her to meet my wife."

"Ini!" he called.

She came along, and voices began to buzz about Anne, her beauty, her outfit, her husbandry; yet the same voice did not leave out reportage on recalcitrance and poverty manifested through people's outfit. Nonetheless, we enjoyed ourselves. Anne testified to that, and she made some friends among the group of women who have been christened passport wives. They were shipped to their husbands from the village.

You may wonder why, but that was the trend. Our men chose not to marry the African women they saw in America; they did not dare marry those born in America; they said they have lost their ways; they have become Americanized, and they said that simply to say that the women were unruly, free, liberated, and reckless. So, they flew home to marry those women they deemed submissive; "village virgins" they called them; the circumcised, and it was easy for them because any woman at home will rush to marry any man from America, even if he did not have a face.

That was the trend then, and with that came a new sensibility, a new way of life that coupled with, among other things, deceit, lust, and arrogance. Their stories abound, and they were common among all storytellers and as an illustrative rebuke; but this one was spectacular, the epitome of all that could be wrong.

Chimuanya, one of these younger groups of men that came after us, felt the wind of marriage. I did not know him; I heard his story. He was thirty then, and all of his friends were married and had children; consequently, they had little or no time for him. To patch things up, he killed himself with work, darting from his regular job as a certified nursing assistant to driving a cab. When the wind came, he made inquiries; he was really afraid that time would overtake him and turn him into an impotent bachelor. Next, he flew home to sample the women, who fell like withered lilies on his feet and believed him, and answered to his whims. They were impressed with him.

"What do you do there?" Agnes asked him. She was among the women most men from America had sampled; she had Bachelor of Science degree in Chemistry and Biology; yet no one married her. She was not ugly; as the stories went, she knew so much about America. The truth, though, was that her university classmate, with whom she had a fire, was in America, and they were in touch. He gave her more advantage over the other girls whom she dwarfed with her American antics.

"I am a doctor," Chimuanya lied, but he impressed Agnes more, and she turned into an angelic being of indescribable nature, acting beyond all Chimuanya's expectations. In addition,

Chimuanya saw her academic degrees, which topped her willingness to please him. He thought of what he could become; what she could study; having found an answer, he started rushing his parents to begin the marriage rituals. He even opted to pay off some of the processes. All the same, Agnes herself thought of the possibilities on her road to Elysium.

Well! They got married, and she came to America. Her experiences were not radically different from Anne's. What made them different was the belief that her husband was a doctor, and there was no way she could have found out easily. Each morning, he would leave the house in white attire, with a stethoscope around his neck, in a spic and span Mercedes truck; he would not come back until late like other doctors, even though he actually left his morning nursing job to rent a taxi. She had no circumstance to find out; Chimuanya enrolled her in nursing school, so she became engrossed in it, and it offered Chimuanya an opportunity to moonlight as a real doctor as he rehearsed with her Anatomy and Physiology, Pharmacology, Drug Calculation and Diseases. In all, Chimuanya was always high with what he expected from his wife's education. He bragged about it, and some people whose wives were not nurses envied him, and often tempted themselves with the dream, and at times at the peril of a broken heart and loss of hope. These same people did not know that Agnes did not know about Chimuanya's jobs. Their reactions towards her studies were curious. She thought. She did not do anything about it, though.

On the day of her graduation, Chimuanya, in complete excitement, forgot his plot. He threw a party for her, and those in attendance were mostly cab drivers, and they came from their work. Their comportment was unbecoming of doctors; their language was inordinate; they were verbose, and constantly referred to the onslaught of money that would come Chimuanya's way, the nearby transformation. Agnes wondered. She felt she had become a victim to all the stories she heard about America. A disconnection began to exist between them in spite of the money Chimuanya dreamed she would bring through her job. It did not come easy though; Chimuanya pretended that he had extended his hours in the hospital, and urged Agnes to pull double-triple shifts. Money flowed; they bought a huge house, but were very rarely in it, except when they slept. Agnes then involved her classmate, who dug up everything about Chimuanya. She then opened her Pandora box. She played along. Now she began pretending that she was doing double-triple shifts. She measured Chimuanya' schedules; she was able to predict his departures and arrivals. In between them, she occupied herself with other men. Next, she became pregnant for one of them. The story spread like wildfire. Chimuanya disappeared; some people said he became disembodied. A different portion came to Agnes; she was torn in-between the freedom she exercised with her pregnancy and her sense of the ancestors, the people, her people; the wind of freedom was more infernal than the silent and distant rebuke of the ancestors. Another story spawned out of her *predicament*, that she could engage men with abandon because she was uncircumcised, that the men who went to her only wanted to experiment the uncircumcised. She *is* now an ambiguous reference, for no one *knows* what she *thinks* of herself.

Elo, other passport wives ran their husbands out of the house, and pushed them down the vale of tears where there was gnashing of teeth. I think I am blessed.

Elo smacked secretly.

\* \* \*

On the following day, I left for work having perched a kiss on her lips. Altogether, she became lonely, like a river without a fish, not through speech though, but for lack of presence that's meant to distract, annihilating solitude and loneliness. But, she was lonely, filled with thought, which she naively tackled without solution. Then the phone rang.

"Who is speaking?"

"It is Ini."

"Ini?"

"Emma's wife."

"Oh! I'm sorry. Now, I remember. How are you?"

"I'm fine. How about you?"

"Fine."

"What are you doing?"

"Nothing, just sitting here."

"You are not even watching television."

"I'm tired of it now."

"Tired? That's your sitter."

"Welll!"

"You could get out, you know, do something."

"No."

They talked for another two hours, circling affairs that bothered them very little.

"Do you go to school yet?" Anne asked.

"I have finished my nursing program. I work now, I do night shift; at times, I do double, but I am off today."

"That's nice."

"Are you going to school?"

"Not yet, but I will start nursing next semester."

"That's good. Wait! Turn on your television. Channel four," Ini requested.

"What's in it?"

"You will find out."

It was a talk-show on teenage pregnancy. Three thirteen years old girls were in the panel, and defiantly defended their motherhood without vouchsafing the knowledge of who the fathers of their babies were. They were happy, almost fulfilled, but with little education, and they found their reasons as just the desire to be called moms.

"Is this how it is over here?" Anne said with perplexity.

"That's how my sister."

"It is terrible."

"They are not saying that."

"They don't have to. One who perpetrates an odious act does not have to see it as such. It may be a solemnity of all he is. Yet, it is odious."

"That's true."

For another hour, they were still on the phone. But Anne was feeling refreshed like a watered earth. Her day felt good, and she looked forward to another, hoping to talk to Ini some more. She cherished it; and like that, her boredom thinned away; like that her loneliness disappeared, even though she was alone; like that her sense of decorum diminished, and very seldom did she consider it.

On a certain day, after I have left for work, and as was my wont, I perched a kiss on her lips, I thought that everything was the same. But when I came home, I was attended by confusion, plus the fatigue of the day; a turmoil of spirit beset me and dragged me along with menace. There was no food on the table; the stove was cold; and she was talking on the telephone.

"Anne! Anne!" I called. She did not hear me.

"Anne!" I called again.

"Oh! I'll call you back. He is here."

"He can't stop you from talking on the phone," the voice said.

"I know, but he is here."

I was famished, and the muscles of my stomach contracted with hunger; it was painful because I had expected her to have some food for me.

"Did you cook something?" I asked, wondering.

"No," she responded. "I was tired," she added with utter indifference.

\* \* \*

Elo was amazed at the story now. More so, she was amazed at what she thought was Nkem's puerility, his lack of manhood, his inability to make his wife do want he wanted. Altogether, she was amazed that Anne would opt for such negligence, dirtying her womanhood, her domesticity, that emblem of her nubility, for no one would have looked at her if she did not have it. But her amazement is not mine. To be amazed about a woman is a sort of delusion. I know what a woman is. I will not tell you any lie; I am a woman: A woman is a fruitful figure, which represents unhappiness when she bewails herself, when she spurns an affair; then she becomes a vermin, a leech, creeping with kamikaze, and dragging everything by her neighborhood to a perfunctory exorcism if not to uncalled suicide. They may cry of the virgin mother to vouchsafe their sweetness; yet, I know Jezebeel; I know Ruth, too; I know Wife of Bathe; I know the attic woman. But, Nkem did not know.

"What did you do after that? Did you just keep silent?" Elo

asked, very much perturbed. Her eyes were quizzical like a hound's.

"Nothing really. But I could not have done anything."

"You should have sent her home. That's how it is done; when a woman is not true to her bride prize."

"I could not have done that. So much was involved being in America. I only readjusted and prayed that the school may open that she may go and learn some thing else; perhaps the confusion out there."

At this juncture, Nkem's enthusiam for his reportage reached its peak. He neither bathed none of his eyes nor tingled his feet, nor cracked his knuckled. He assumed the figure of an old man who fed little children at his feet with stories and parables; at times mingled with peculiar meaning; at times merely laughable; at times self-searching and invigorating, filled with drama. Yet, he continued.

There was topsy-turvy the first day she went to school, though to my joy. People, men and women, roamed around, very quickly like roaches on a hot pan, very serious, moving from building to building with loads of their books hung fashionably on their backs. Anne was among them. I was happy; and I was scared too, for I feared that some men might start running after her. And she never failed to tell whenever they did, because she laughed at them, especially for their inquiry regarding her culture and mannerism, what she termed their dwarf awareness. Well! She kept going. Slowly, she grew comfortable with being among a throng of people, administering their joke and naivety, their gibberish countenance of reality, vulgarism. She learned and assimilated like a black sheep in the dark. Then she made friends. Three girls. All nursing students. Kimberly, the oldest of them all was twenty-six. She had two daughters, thirteen and twelve. Next was Phina, twenty-five, and Tiffany, twenty-four, with a ten-year old boy.

They reminded me of Ashley, but they were not as beautiful. Phina was churlish. Kimberly was fat with a pig face; Tiffany, lanky. They were an amusing triad for the cause they ran, celebration of womanhood. It was on account of this cause that they approached Anne initially. As she told me that day; she had just finished her class on a very quiet day, and was on her way home when they approached her. Anne was calm with her peculiar walk, almost wobbling.

"Hello!" Tiiffany said smiling

"Hello!" Anne replied. Tiffany was startled. She realized her intonation.

"I am Tiffany."

"I am Anne."

"You are doing nursing, right?"

"Yes," Anne replied.

"I have seen you in my class," Tiffany replied.

"You have accent," Kimberly added. "Where are you from?"

"Africa," she replied like all Africans.

"Are you from Olinka?"

They looked at themselves and darted aside an empathy that left Anne confused.

"Something wrong?" Anne asked with a furrowed brow.

"No we are wondering if you are among the circumcised African women. We know Africans are circumcised," Tiffany said, reminiscing on recent propaganda on the essence of female body, the elegance of the vulva, mutilation and barbarism; she also reminisced on the errors that is Africa, at least, as she heard through the propaganda. How tamed must she be, Tiffany thought. How docile, how partitioned, she must be.

"Are you circumcised?"

"Of course, I am," Anne replied.

"Oh! Another mutilated woman."

"Mutilation? That's your belief. That's the way to womanhood. Nobody will marry you if you are not circumcised. By the way, how come you have argument about a phenomenon from which you are separated both by culture and language? Anne asked.

"Walker got it all."

"Who is Walker?"

"Alice Walker. Here." She dished out a copy of *Possessing the Secret of Joy* and gave her. She had also *Warrior Marks.*

"Read it."

"I don't understand."

"Read it. I will see you in class."

Anne departed, and very faintly understood what transpired among them.

* * *

Anne came home with the book. I shuddered because I have read it. I saw its drift, outlawing of a custom. I shuddered further because I did not know how to address the question she might ask, how to deal with her new and false knowledge. Nonetheless, she devoured the book like a sumptuous feast. Some passages she read aloud to me, laughing, some she mumbled: 'Circumcision,' She whispered. What exactly is the procedure? She asked briskly. I was reminded of a quality I did not like at all. Bluntness. Or is it? A going to the heart of the matter even if it gave everyone concerned a heart attack. '...Some cultures demand excision of only the clitoris, others insisted on a thorough scraping away of the genital area.... Everyone knew that if a woman was not circumcised her unclean part would grow so long they'd soon touch her thighs. That's true. Certainly to all my friends who had been circumcised, my uncircumcised vagina was thought of as monstrosity. They laughed at me.'

"Nkem," she shouted at that point.

"I am here," I said.

She continued reading: 'each human being from the first was endowed with two souls of different sex, or rather with two principles corresponding to two distinct regions. In the man, the female soul was located in the prepuce; in the woman, the male soul was in the clitoris. The dual soul is a danger; a man should be a man, and a woman female. That's the beauty of circumcision.'

"Have you read this book?"

"I have. Just mythic lies!"

"Lies? Why would somebody ask me to read it? See the references."

"Who asked you to?"

"My friend, Tiffany."

"Did she tell you that circumcision is not peculiar to Africa, that America used it as instrument of power on the slaves, and as a prescription for hysteria among women? Did she then respond by saying that African slaves brought that with them, that it is African phenomenon, what Africans do to control their women? If that were true, I would be more concerned with the curiosity of America in *examining* the slaves. Did she give you the gospel of Barnabas, where Jesus tells the story of the origin of circumcision?" I dashed into my library and pulled out a text, flipping through its pages. He read: 'Leave fear to him that hath not circumcised his foreskin, for he is deprived of paradise.' The Israelites had to be circumcised before they join Joshua's army against the Palestine. There is no certainty on the origin," I said to challenge to the text.

"Walker is not worried about origin or who practices it; she is worried about the evil," she rebutted.

"I knew that," I said to myself. Then, I shut up, scared for what might be her next question.

"Are they circumcised like us?" She asked.

"How would I know?"

"But their clitorises have not grown like a penis."

"Do you wonder why you are so gentle? Do you wonder why they are not? It is circumcision."

She glared at me. A new impression appeared on her face. She was agape. She said nothing, but her eyes were transparent with wonder and a turmoil that befalls one who had flirted with death. In silence, she walked to the bedroom.

"It is all lies, Anne, filled with contradictions, no certainty; it is intellectual," I said behind her.

"You are better with circumcision," I continued. But she paid me no mind; and the attention she gave me then was foreign, barren of all I know about her, filled with distance and a little despair. I sought to link the distance with romance.

The following day, she turned the book back to Tiffany who showed her happiness, a happiness that spread among the triad as they believed that Anne have joined their cause. However, she followed with skepticism and loaded them with questions.

"Do you hate circumcision?"

"Why do you hate it?"

"What is the difference in having it and not having it?"

"Don't you think Walker has told lies?"

Tiffany squinted.

Yet, deep in Anne's soul, there was an affirmation of what she read, what she felt, a difference, a little repudiation of herself.

# 6

There's a fly on the sore in my spirit now. It fattens itself with the mucus that oozes out from my sore. I want to kill it. I fan the sore to blow it away. It basks to the gust of the wind from my blow. I want to kill it, to hit on it with my palm. But I may hurt myself too. But the fly will be dead. I want to kill it. I am raising my hand now. Slowly I have measured. I am landing my hand now. No! It is not a fly. It is a woman. What is she doing there? No! It is not a woman. It is my story. My story. It is now eating deep into my spirit, killing me so that it may live. Let it be. Let no benevolent spirit fight it. Let it kill me as long as it lives. Who am I in the presence of my story, where a woman wonders about herself, where women exploit what they don't understand, where a woman wonders how good she is brought up? It's been men's question, in which their sincerity is short of truth; in which they presuppose a thralldom, a life in the kitchen, a scream in the bedroom, children. But is it true?

What do you understand when a woman queries the goodness

of another? Isn't division? What really makes a woman? A state of mind? Is anybody born a woman? Or born a man? Judgment is yours. Let the fly live.

And Nkem stood up. Having walked around, he continued. His tone was lined with emotion. My house was like a beehive, always buzzing with noises. Phina, Tiffany, and Kimberly were always there, discussing nothing but child birth. For Anne had become pregnant. They traded their knowledge with abandon.

"Do you know what it's going to be?"

"No," Anne replied.

"You could find out."

"I don't want to. Call Nkem please?"

"Kem," Tiffany called, at the same time, instructing her that they don't depend on men.

"I have two girls," she continued like that. "Their father is not even around, and I don't care anymore than they do."

Anne laughed. Without amazement. Their friendship had gotten a bizarre rapport, such we speak of palm oil and salt. They were amicable to each other; visited each other's home, and joked and played. But what they had in common at that time I could not fathom. One day, Anne visited Kimberly having been twice at Tifanny's and Phina's. Her stomach was then well bulged, big like a head of palm fruit; she dragged, almost like an elephant. When she arrived at Kimberly's, her two daughters rushed at her. They were happy to see her, and more so because she was pregnant; one was blonde, busty, with oozing rusticity, lascivious, loose and wanton; the other was dark, tender, coquettish, and passionate.

"When are you due," one said.

"In a month."

"Is it a girl?"

"I don't know."

"Mom! I want to have a baby."

"Are you going to raise it?" Kimberly entered with a little agony.

"She is not old enough to have a baby," Anne said, flushed with amazement that Kimberly entertained her child speaking of childbirth.

"That's not true," Kimberly joined. "I had them when I was around their age."

Anne looked around, a little nonplused, a little boggled, but deep in her soul was a complete dissatisfaction, which if laid bare would appear with the grotesqueness of a morning ghost. She looked on.

"Where is their father?" she asked later.

"He is not here," Kimberly said.

"I shall baby sit for you, aunt Anne," one of the children said.

"Me too," the other added.

"Yeah! because I said so."

"I shall smack your face."

"I smack you to, thank you very much."

They ran around with annoying persistence, obeying no rules, doing what they wanted without chastisement. Kimberly screamed at them from a distance paying little attention to what they did.

"Stop girls," she said like a fire suffering a cool shower. Her seriousness was wanting like an illusion, a mirage, a mockery. Nonetheless, she talked with Anne of nothing but motherhood, of course. It irritates me to remember.

One night. Nine months had gone. I barely survived it. She came towards me one quiet evening pointing at her stomach. Her face was writhed. I looked; fluid was traveling down her thighs. Pain stood on her face, so heavy was it that it did not allow her to scream or speak. I bundled her into the car and rushed off to the hospital; and she was made to lay before strangers whom she flashed with her anatomy. They wore a strange look on their faces. Her vagina was not familiar to them. It fascinated them. She screamed.

Did you say scream? Elo asked. That's not done. A woman does not scream while she gives birth. And you have no business being there. It is the work of the woman, a midwife.

"Well, it wasn't that day."

People will surely talk about her in the market place if she were to give birth like that here, Elo observed.

It is not the same. They gathered before her, filled with expectation.

"Push!" they yelled like a crowd dragging a truck up a hill.

"Push!"

"Push!"

"Push!"

The baby's head stuck out; its shoulder followed; his torso came. My face radiated with joy. I have never felt like that before. I thought about nothing but joy. I smiled. Then its legs came tied together with the umbilical cord. Gently, the doctor severed it and placed the baby on Anne's arm. She smiled while tears welled up in her eyes, and slowly traveled down her temple as she held my hand.

"What's her name?" the nurse asked.

"Tracy."

"Are you going to circumcise her?" one nurse asked taking the baby from her and reminiscing on her fascinating vagina.

We answered variedly; she answered no.

"It is up to you," the nurse said. "But I don't think it is advisable," she added and left.

"Why shouldn't we circumcise her, Anne?"

"Why should we? We don't have to continue with that lie now. Do we?"

"It is the book. Isn't it?"

"It is reality more than the book."

We differed and Tracy was never circumcised.

"What?" Elo screamed.

"She's not circumcised."

"Tell me no more." She rose to leave. But she turned back because she could not contain herself, thinking that she was dreaming.

"What is it that she is not circumcised? People are thrown into bondage because of that."

"That's my fear, but hear me out?"

"Hear you out? Do you know that she is a taboo; she is not even a woman yet."

"I should believe, Elo. But the place where she was born is not like here."

"No, you did not stand your feet firmly on the ground."

"I did, but the convention favored the opposite."

"She is not a woman yet, that's all I say."

"In what way? Tell me."

"Customarily. I wonder if the king will let her son marry her."

"I don't know."

"Tell me also that you did not circumcise Troy?"

"He was circumcised."

"He was."

That is not the only thing. She grew up around Kimberly's children who babysat her, who played with her and thought her their games. She is wayward. I can't discipline her because her mother has distorted my discipline. My words are like a balloon, filled with air and without weight, like water poured on a rock.

She was the epitome of her mother's recalcitrance; every bit of her mother's action resounded in her voice and affirmation. I emaciated for lack of peace of mind. I wobbled in my clothes; my look changed. I wanted to slap their faces. But I could not. I would not. But the thirst to do so grew up in me like a watered seedling, trudging on my skin with defiance.

"Let me tell you," Elo entered furiously, "Your wife is growing tentacles. I know her before you married her. There was simplicity about her which every man sought. And that's why she was found for you. She has gone mad with being a 'thick madam,' as though she doesn't go to latrine. And Tracy is a wild animal; until she is trained, you shall know no peace; you will not rest. Tell me, where is the woman who can walk away uncircumcised? Where is the woman that challenges the authority of his husband? Where is a child who neglects his chores or repudiates the strokes of his father's correction and punishment? What you have is a disease that afflicts one who's in contact with western culture. When we were growing up, life was fruitful, yet we were marked lashes for our omissions. Nkem, there is a reason for everything. Don't worry, when the wind blows we shall see the buttocks of chickens."

"Daddy," Troy called, coming from the house. He turned toward him. He looked worried. He motioned him to come. He did; he picked him up in his arms. Not long after that, Ifeoma came in with a bunch of firewood tie together with sheaves of leaves. She had them balanced on her head and walked majestically. He saw them, greeted them, but paid them no mind. Troy ran after her while she entered the kitchen. She offloaded them and began to separate the sheaves from the woods.

"What are you doing with the bush?" Troy inquired.

"It is not bush, Troy. The goats eat it," she replied.

"The goat?"

"Yes."

"You cut the bush for the goats."

"Yes. I'll you show you. Just as man doesn't eat everything, goats don't eat everything. They eat some and not others."

"How do you know? You are not a goat."

"I just know. Every animal eat palm frond. Watch this." She tied the sheaves together with palm fronds and took it to the goat. She hung it in the mid air, not high so that the goats might not stretch their neck; and not too low either. She hung it, and it dangled like pendulum. Simultaneously, the goat grabbed it, first the palm frond.

"Waow!" Troy said.

"This is cool," he said again.

"Do you do that in America?"

"No. I have never seen a goat there. Daddy buys meats, burger, that's all."

"This is cool," he replied.

"Now, you've seen one."

"Feeding the goat makes you African, right?"

"No."

"What makes you African? Tell me."

Ifeoma paused and looked at him. She was boggled for she had never thought about the question. Yet, she did not want to answer in order not to lead him astray. But deep in her heart she knew that being African is far more than feeding the goat.

"Am I African? Do you think?" Troy queried.

"Yes, you are," Ifeoma replied softly. The answer surprised him, and he rushed to his father filled with joy.

"Daddy I'm African, Ifeoma said I'm African."

"Of course, you are," Nkem replied. In amazement, he looked at Elo like a wounded animal. But she said nothing.

# BOOK 2

# 1

Another day came just like any other day. The sun slowly came from the thick cloud that was as dark as bitumen in the azure, 'sirened' by a slightly cool gust of wind. It was not menacing; it was gentle and soothing. Trees enjoyed it, and they danced to it like in a festival, shouting in whistling voices. Men did the same while grazing their sheep, which bleated randomly, expressing dissatisfaction with their pasture. Then Marcel left his house in his baggy trousers that was pulled up to his armpit with a grayish suspender, a white cotton T-shirt and a black pair of shoes. He entered his father's car, which he left him before he died; he drove to Nkem's house.

He knew Nkem as a child. They even combed the streets together in search of 'cunts' as they used to say. What a way to describe women! He knew him in America too. They went to different schools; and while Nkem studied medicine, Marcel studied fine arts. He taught drama in the college.

When he arrived, Nkem, Anne, and Elo were at the porch, soaking the gentle breeze. There was a distinction in their faces, though; one marked with peace and joy while the other's marked with inimical distance that was present, not by merely looking at it but by listening to its voice that was snappy, roaring, and dry. It lacked splendor and good report.

"You know Marcel?" Nkem said, clearing the ground for an eventual introduction.

"Of course, I know him," Elo replied.

"He is a faggy, that's all," Anne added with a want of splendor in her tone.

"What's a faggy?" Elo inquired. They laughed, wondering how to present an explanation.

"Mom, Troy is going to the bush with Ifeoma," Tracy reported from the rear.

"What!" Anne stood up frenetic.

"He said he is going to the bush with Ifeoma to get firewood and goat leaves," Tracy roared further, her jugular vein stood out, large and fragile.

"I don't believe this. Is this what you taught him yesterday?"

"Let the child be!" Nkem added.

"Be! What if the snake bites him?"

"Has the snake bitten Ifeoma?"

"Ifeoma knows where to go," Elo entered.

"Shut up! Nobody asked you."

"You should not talk like that to her, Anne," Nkem said.

Meanwhile, Marcel approached them and sat down quietly, seeing how rioted their faces were.

"What's up Nkem?" he said.

"Not a damn thing," he replied. He was furious, looking at Troy run after Ifeoma, screaming "bye bye" to them.

"Let's go, mom," Tracy entered. She was in clothes that made her look lascivious.

"Where to?" Nkem asked.

"To my husband's"

"In those things?" Elo wondered.

Nonetheless, they left. Behind them the air was tough, hard to breathe, like a stone. Marcel silently darted here and there, seeking comportment, a haven. He adjusted in his seat.

"Is she married now?" he said.

"No. She is only excited that Maduka will marry her," Nkem replied.

"Those whose palm kernels are cracked by the benevolent spirits should not forget to be humble. Mmm! Marriage! I was married once. Nkem you knew about it."

Elo stuck her fingers into her ears disabling herself to hear. But Marcel continued emptying his past with utter temerity, lamenting his ways with women.

"Sometimes, the tenderness you seek in a woman will be possessed by a man; sometimes the care you require from a woman will be well given by a man; and the way you want to be loved came from a man. What will stop you from following that man. You know Nkem, 'distinction does not consist in the facile docility to conventions, but in being numbered among those who are true, honest, pure, lovely.' There is parochialism in the sanctioned manner of loving, man and woman. There is slavery there, trepidation of women, the show of masculine intrepidity, patriarchy. I'm glad I went to America, because I would not have known."

"You are filled with taboos," Elo said with anger, itching to leave them.

"That's liberation, Elo. People do it here too. Women do it. They might do it out of love, frustration, or what they believe they have lost; but you wont hear about it."

"You are lying, and even if they do, they will not be condoned," Elo added.

"That's a lie. I know different people."

"They must have all been to America."

"Not at all."

"Don't bring it up around me again, or I shall call the elders. We cannot condone that. Do you know what you do to our women? They shall grow old without husbands, without children."

All this time, Nkem was silent like a humble spectator, listening to them, but bored and lethargic. His face paled and was dotted with despair, which was spectacular, very visible, as the sun had appeared in the sky. It was a little hot, with creepy voices of insect rising with rays of the sun; a distant shout of a mother after her child. Then Troy came back with Ifeoma carrying a dwarf load of firewood on his head.

"Dad, see what I got," he said. Nkem looked and saw a miniature bunch of firewood on his head. He waved at him and smiled; at the same time, he sought for energy to make Elo understand Marcel. He explained what he understood by Marcel's action, a choice of life, a transvaluation of reality, a counter culture, a season of anomie, absurdism, madness, the birth of tragedy, excision of tradition, death, yet the exuding of life. In all, he did not chastise Marcel.

"You are all filled with taboos. That's what America crowned you with. I know you before you left," she said.

"It is not a taboo," Marcel said after all.

\* \* \*

Anne and Tracy had not reached the king's palace; the sun was in the center of the sky, baring everything with hot and sizzling rays, and scorching them. The king was, however, in the porch of his house, surrounded by flamboyant shrubs, which had formed a cozy resort. He was shoveling with the back-side of his right thumb mountains of ground tobacco into his noses. He scooped an amount as big as an anthill from his left palm where he had poured the amount he wanted. His nostrils were stuffed with it; his mouth was open as he gasped for air.

"His Highness," a man came, an old man, older than he was. He had a cloth tied around his waist. His body was bare and dotted with over-aged hair, waiting to be nourished. He was barefooted. His head was bald, making his bushy grayish eyebrows distinct and horrible.

"Albert," the king greeted.

He sat down, dusted his hand and put out the left one immediately for some tobacco. Slowly, and like the king, he shoveled some amount into his nose.

"Who prepare your tobacco?" he asked gasping for air.

"My brother's wife."

"Etuodi?"

"Yes."

"She knows her work."

For a moment, he took his eyes away from his palm. He saw Anne and Tracy entering the palace.

"Who are these people?" Albert inquired in a lowered voice.

"That's my friend's, Maduka's family. The little one is his grandchild. Maduka shall marry her."

"Your son! Oh!" he remembered. "Why is she dressed like that? Will she ever be able to bear a child?"

"Your Highness," Anne greeted.

"Your Highness," Tracy did the same.

They passed on. Albert rose, frenetic, almost anguished. His body shook with a borrowed envy. His eyes darted, and his eyebrows stood up. He sighed heavily like a snake and began effortlessly with a voice filled with torture.

"You don't greet me. I am not the king. Children of today. You don't even know me. Why not? Why not? You cast your eyes up to the sky." He was filled with bitterness. But they were astonished.

"What's that, your Highness? Did we do something wrong?" Anne asked, coming back.

"Did you do something wrong? That's what you say. Do you know who I am."

"No. Who are you sir," Anne asked with sarcasm.

"We went with your husband's father to your house when you were married. I tapped your father's palm wine. I farmed his land, all."

Infuriated, Anne left.

"Children of today!" Albert added.

Meanwhile, Maduka was talking with his mother in her room. She had vowed not to let him forget for an instant the step that he was trying to make through marriage, never to leave himself to the possibility of peace in marriage; and never to leave himself neither to the impossibility of peace. Maduka wanted to cry. He feared.

"What's the need of marriage then?" Maduka asked.

"It is life my son. There is the birth of man and his suffering, which when he survives he becomes a full man. No man has suffered who is not married. You know we women are pigs, even though we don't acknowledge that. But we know."

"I think I'm too young anyway."

"Young! You have reached the age of manhood, Maduka."

"How can you say so?"

"I know."

"How can I get used to this? There is always something dreadful about it. I never said I wanted to get married yet."

He was trembling with agitation.

"You will be fine. We know what is best for you."

"I think I'm not ready."

"How come? This is the part of my life I have been waiting for," she replied, her eyes dilated with perplexity, like a monster who suddenly lost its monstrosity, who has been tamed, who stared at its diabolic deeds and for the first time saw their evil content. Soon, a kind of quietness grew about them. Maduka wondered at it. He knew that he would marry, at least, to obey his parents, to do what they wanted. He did not hesitate in his mind, but there was a peculiar kind of knitting of his brows, such that appeared when he was pensive with thought.

"Do you want to say something?" she asked.

"No."

A knock fell on the door.

"Tracy and her mother are here," the servant announced.

"They are here, and don't bring shame on us," she said and left the room to attend to her prospective in-laws.

Albert was shoveling the last mountain of tobacco into his nose. Next, he cleared his throat as though he wanted to say something. He got relaxed in the chair, rather, filled with anticipation. It was then three o'clock. Like him Tracy was in the house filled with anticipation, waiting for Maduka to come and see her. She bubbled with joy, as she knew that he would come. Then, he came and took her.

"What are we going to do?" she said.

"I don't know."

"Take me to the town."

"Town?"

"Yes." She took his hand and swung it around her neck. Slowly, Maduka removed it, blushing.

"All right! Let's go to the town."

"Bye mom! I see you at home later," she said and followed Maduka.

They left, walking side by side. Tracy took his right hand again and swung it around her shoulder.

"Leave it there," she said while he was trying to remove it. He was nervous, however.

"Your Highness," she greeted on their way out. But the king did not hear her for his eyes were locked at the hand that was hanging on her shoulder.

"Take your hand off her shoulder, Maduka," the king said with little agony.

"A taboo shall soon be committed in your house," Albert entered.

Maduka was chagrined, however. He removed his hands, which he never enjoyed leaving on her shoulder. His eyes took the effect of a chasm as he walked along with her. They embarked in a car. Maduka's soul was clinging away from Tracy's precipitancy; but she laughed her way through the town, shooting questions Maduka merely answered in the affirmative; yet guided by a form of forgetfulness that co-existed with an elaborate desire, a disguised pain.

When they reached the town, they disembarked and trekked for a while talking amidst the throng of people that roamed around.

"Let's get married next week," Tracy said rollicking with the presence of a joy she had manufactured.

"O no! It cannot be done."

"Cannot be done? Why not?"

"There are some customary things that need to be done first. I still have to pay the pride price."

"For what? You are not buying me."

"It is the custom."

They walked around the town more. Some of the people who were also outdoors that day saw them and heard their conversation, her precipitancy, which distracted them from their affairs, selling palm oil, measuring food with a dwarf cup; they noted the ecstatic terrain of her voice, charged with some authority that's reposed for demons; her comportment was alien, and it made the people wonder who she was until she jotted into little laughs given by a woman who has won a man from all other women. But they took her with a pinch of salt, inquiring where she came from. But her affection for Maduka then was a sort of being, a presence; it took to a pedestal of radiation, an oblivion of her past sorrow and gloom, doubt and fear, all perpetrated by men. They might be approaching; they might be going away, but he did not know.

Next, they entered the car and left. Tracy was boisterous while she observed to Maduka's dismay the crudeness of the people that passed them by, their manners which she said lacked spices of gentility; their clothes which she disliked for their atavistic leaning. The sight did her no good for she saw how aloof she could be among them, how different she was from them. Then she grew restless like boiling water; everything was turning into a bore; the little left was her hope to be with Maduka. That's what she thought until they came to a field, a field faraway with fresh green grasses gently growing, struggling to outgrow each other, to be more green. Immediately, pleasantness returned to their journey; one very apparent from Tracy's face, which had melted with emotion and smiles that lingered abundantly on her lips.

Again, they came out of the car and walked some yards of the field.

"I have not been here before," Maduka said.

"Why not?"

"I guess it is somebody's land."

"It is romantic, Maduka. I wish we had a camera."

They walked further, but stopped suddenly because some insects began to bite them. She cried and begged to be taken home. Nonetheless, she was angry, burrowing a hell in her soul for the insects for they had disturbed a romance she was cultivating in his mind, a romance in the field where she believed her sensibility would be well whetted. But her hope was shattered, and she battled with what was left of it.

"Have you been with any girl before?" she asked with petulance.

"No! not at all," Maduka replied.

"You mean you've never had sex."

"We don't do that before marriage," he replied, feeling that his virginity was a form of weakness, feeling some impropriety in his blood because he had loved many girls without sex. He was detached from it, but it was not complicated that he would not want any woman that way; for him, sex was a taboo, an ugly fruit that mars your taste of life forever, an indelible excision from your sense of purity; a thief of time crawling under your skin as a desire, so wild that your life depends on it; a joy though. Maduka, however, believed that nothing was wrong with abstaining from it. But this abstinence, this virginity, became something else, a shattering tremor, a matrix of pain without the proximity of any apothecary.

"Really?" Tracy entered with perplexity. He hesitated.

"But I want to kiss you," Tracy said. Maduka could not speak against the anomaly of that gesture. While his soul was watered with joy that was to come forth, his body resisted, fearing nothing visible but the voices in his head that burdened him with the enthusiasm to deny her, to chastise her and call her names of indignity.

"Do you have to?" Maduka said still humble to his body and soul.

"Yes," she said and threw her hands over his shoulder. Immediately, he was flooded with desire, a paroxysm, which shattered his fears about marriage.

"You know we shall be married one day," he said.

"I do. You shall have and keep me," she replied.

"I suppose."

"Nobody shall put asunder in our union."

"No. Nobody."

"We shall have children," her sensuality began to triumph; and with passion her feeling for him grew. She tightened her grip around his neck and kissed his cheek, where the line of the mouth ended. Something in him shrank. His freshness disappeared. He felt the rocking of her breast with delight. His mind was boggled, but filled with a desire, which he wished he had shared with other women in the past. She linked her hands behind his neck.

"I can kiss you, now," she said. He was petrified with joy; yet he wanted to detest her overarching dominion, her self-expression.

Then, they left, and he took her home.

When he arrived at his home, his father was on the porch cutting roasted meat. He greeted him.

"You look pale, Maduka," his mother observed, passing him on the way.

"What happened on the road today?" she added.

"Nothing."

"You are not telling the truth," she said. Maduka hesitated. His eyes welled up with tears.

"This marriage," he said.

"What of it?"

"Is Tracy really the one for me?"

"We dipped our eyes in the water to find her. She is a beautiful girl."

"I know; at the same time, I wonder If I should really marry her."

"Do you like her or not?"

"I do, but I fear…."

"Fear?"

"Yes, what shall I do? And she seems to be fond of me."

"Become fond of her too, because you are marrying her."

Maduka listened. His mind buckled, and he felt that he had not really thawed the ice that's chilling his body. He perspired in his palms.

"But no one has a good opinion of her, her dress," he added.

"You are listening to the people. Their opinion is like a smoke, always up in the air, disappearing. Do you know what is said of your father and me? Terrible things, but we are still here."

Her presentation of their steadfastness, their adamant disposition to the opinionated people, reassured Maduka. Again, his mind blossomed with satisfaction. He thought of Tracy. Smile traveled through his lips. His face lightened. Laughter came, and his mother laughed too.

In another occasion, Tracy took him to her house. Everybody saw them because it was still day. Elo marveled. Ifeoma could not put her thoughts in words, but her face represented a disturbance hewed out of an unfamiliar spectacle. Tracy showed him her life in pictures: This is me in the zoo; this is Troy; this me, Mom, and Dad; here is my friend; this was my boyfriend in high school. She continued like an anointed egotist. Maduka looked on, but pale and detached.

"Is your boyfriend African?" He asked almost without interest.

"No. He is African-American."

"He looks familiar to me."

"You must have seen his ancestors."

"Where is he from? North or South."

"He was born in New York."

"Is that his home town?"

"No. I don't know his hometown. He lives in Maryland; that's where he pays his taxes."

"What village is he from?"

"What all this questions for?"

"You know Marcel? He said there are no villages in America. I told him no, that they might be calling it something else. No man can live without a village."

"Well I don't know."

At that, they dispersed. Maduka seemed like a hero among his peers, who now envied him, as they believed that he would cross over to manhood. At times, the envy was devilish; at times, it was good and alloyed with a challenge, which piqued Maduka against several odds like being a bad parent or bad husband. All the same, they denied the possibility of the latter because of his father's wealth. As they saw, money sustained marriage. They invaded him, though, with questions concerning his feeling about marriage and at the same time lodged protest against the manners of his fiancée.

"Your father is just marrying for you. You do not suffer for your wife. You have no barn, no goat," one of them said.

"What's wrong with that?" Maduka replied.

"What's wrong with that? Is that what you say? Listen to him; your palm kernel is cracked by somebody."

"You didn't choose your wife, did you?"

"You didn't, I know. She is from America. She was born for you."

"I have a good relationship with my father; his choice is mine," Maduka said.

"I bet your choice is his, too."

"Yes, can you respect that?"

They looked at themselves. They became mute, scratching their heads in despair. Altogether they became apologetic and begged his friendship. Maduka pitied them and dabbled into a tirade, instructing them of the evils of envy, that it kills, and that it stops nothing. "We are born at the same time," he continued. "We grew up together. We should be all one."

"I agree, but soon you will know how a woman smells. Will I ever?"

They laughed, but not with scorn. Maduka took them to his house where they were treated cordially as they partook of some sumptuous foods. They played and left.

On their way home as Maduka was escorting them, just a mile, they encountered their female peers, rippled hair, ashy legs and feet imprisoned in slippers made out of automobile tires. Their faces etched with traces of manual labor. They shouted at each other.

"Look at the one who will be married," one of them said.

"Why are you marrying her anyway," another added.

"Yes, she looks like a harlot, I saw her in the market the other time."

"Stop!" Maduka charged like a lion

"Listen," he continued. "You don't even know her."

"I know she is from America."

"Can she cultivate your land? No."

"Stop, I said," Maduka reiterated.

Silence engulfed them. The weather became still as if it heard Maduka's warning. They breathed largely. Everyone of them. The boys doled sorrow looking at Maduka. The girls were not scared. They laughed in their heart as their eyes glowed with bizarre sensation, distancing Maduka as fickle.

"I shall leave you," he said to the men. Then he turned and walked home. A battle ensued in his soul. And as he walked, he uprooted pebbles on his way without knowing, plucking leaves from the side bushes. Behind him, however, one of the girls brought Tracy down like a basket hung above the fire and searched her through and through. She found nothing. She put it back there hoping that a secret hand would stuff it.

"She needs to be trained," she said finally.

# 2

I now wonder what makes one person different from the other. Why should one person be picked from a crowd? I wonder. Why should one person cherish being one person and not the other? Perhaps, it is something in the person. But we don't have a crystal ball to see what our souls are made of. Being with one person and not the other behooves of a blind sacrifice, a sacrifice of what is not seen. You could be with one; you could love that one unless you believe that there is an aspect of that one which you don't see. Now, when two people are different, we don't wonder of a blind spot, but of the visible spot, that which made them different. He is brown; he is yellow, he is red; he is green; he is quiet; he is loud. But why? I know. One is what one is made of. I might have told a lie now. But look around and see whether all people you know are what they are made of. Are they not what they want to be, what they have chosen to be? Not minding the distastefulness of the choice. Not minding the approbation.

Let me bend my story just a little with a holy allusion. Once the

Israelites, led by Moses, came to the wilderness, running from Pharaoh. Or running for their lives. Their God had led them, but a terrible pain befell them, a torture of the body and soul. They were famished. They sought the God who led them out of Egypt. They sought for Moses, but he had gone up to the mountain. They were forlorn, hopeless. Then, they hoisted their hope on what they saw and believed, an idol. When Moses came and saw them, he was utterly disturbed; he shattered the idol and beseeched thus: "Choose you today whom you shall serve!" Surely, they chose differently; and different fate befell them according to their choices. Death for idol mongers; and happiness and prosperity for those who retained their God. It is never intelligent to deny your tradition, even in a biting time. Nor should you let education present your tradition as a predicament.

\* \* \*

Marcel was living decently as a teacher. He was well-known in the town for his dedication, even. He took his pupil home; bought them presents; took them on trips; hosted parties for them. To be in his class was like a voyage to heaven. On this account, the principal of the school, an old man, a catholic, set a high standard for anyone who would want to be in his class. This included the knowledge of the catholic catechism, the reception of the holy Eucharist, and academic average of alpha. Naturally, the class was filled with sons and daughters of devout Catholics. The school image rose to its zenith; it became overpopulated with bourgeois children who came to school looking fragile like baskets of eggs, a stick of butter in the sun. And they learned greatly, classics; their manners sharpened; and they always looked up to Marcel whose eloquence they treated like religion. With that he achieved heroism. There was no town from which he had no pupil. They revered him.

"He's like a second father to me."

"He is interesting."

"He is a great teacher."

Gods would envy him of such superlatives; yet he was no less than a god for them because he transmuted their dull minds with a sharp rocket that collapsed every sort of idolatry into a wise and spirited organ. Their manners took a touch of probity. They spoke differently from the array of children from different schools. Their English had alien drawl, which simultaneously camouflaged their wantonness.

"Good morning sir," the class roared as he entered the classroom one quiet morning. He was dressed in bowtie. He was clean; his eyes were pulsating with rustic innocence and did not expect any divergence from his students; but there was another set of eyes, which were not ostensible, which diverged from his student with a sight in his soul of bawdy and lewd character, castrating as a butcher's knife. He climbed the podium with tomes of books under his arms; he set them on the desk that was sullied with chalky substance, a duster, and debris of chalk. There was no sound until he cleaned the blackboard with a duster. Intelligence took up its place there mingled with a concerned enthusiasm. The students watched as they had already been swallowed by his mere presence, digesting what he said with joy, and were ready to do so forever without a turn of mien, seeking substance.

But he continued, raising his right hand, which was ashy with chalk. At the same time, he was confronted with the dust that had risen in the air.

"This is another day, a good day," he began in a voice dragging with pedagogy. "Remember, 'no learning by rote' is my motto. Treat everything with skepticism, not to deny them; but like Descartes, you remember, pause your judgment of acceptance or denial until you have verified. Doubt is a stepping-stone to wisdom. Through doubt you become a sublime one. Doubt and doubt, but learn through your doubt. Do not, however, become Thomases: *video est credo* ; no.

"This is another day, another class. We are still looking at Aeschylus."

"Who is the rival to Aeschylus in Greek drama?" he asked. Silence prevailed.

"Titus," he said, pointing at one boy. He was fifteen.

"Homer," he replied.

"Any objection? Ephraim," he pointed at another boy.

"I am objecting not because Homer was not really a rival to Aeschylus. Homer was an epic poet, who staged the affairs of gods and men. And again, he was known to have existed; you cannot establish the period of his poems, for instance, *Iliad*, when it was written. Such lack of information creates a problem in relating Homer to Aeschylus. I should say that Aeschylus is post-Homer; that Homer is naive; he invokes the Apollonian folk culture as a dream artist. If we shall speak of rivalry, it should be between Homer and Archilochus. One is objective, the other is subjective."

"Ephraim, I will pause on the question of objectivity and subjectivity now. The question remains on rivalry.

"Euripides, Sophocles," Ephraim added.

"Why? Let a girl answer."

There was silence. Notes shuffled like waves slowly hitting the shore as the students fished for the answers in them. Several girls shrank to a specious caricature, heads bent in their notes, the onslaught of knowledge.

"I have the answer," one girl raised her voice.

"Let see what you have, woman," Marcel said.

"It is Aeschylus' use of opposition, a coalescence of two opposing cultures. But in Euripides, there is aesthetic socratism."

I always think that women are comic beings, he thought, looking at her, waiting for her to finish.

"What is the main opposition in Aeschylus? We said it the other day. Charles."

Apollonian and Dionysian votaries," Charles replied.

"Well said Charles. And speaking of opposition, what is it that unites the dramatists, if any?"

"Their genre," another woman entered.

"What is it?"

"Tragedy," she said.

Yes! Tragedy! That's what it is, determined by the presence of the hero who makes a mistake, who dies, whose death leaves us with pity. But there is another tragedy, the tragedy of self-immolation, self-annihilation through the subscription to the spirit of time. Ancient tragedy is no longer performed for education; it is for its establishment. More so, it is far removed from here. I know you are thinking of what I said the other day about representation. How much reality is there in the ancient drama? Does it present us with stories or life, however modulated? Are we not looking at the moonlighting of the author's imagination, his madness, perhaps? Are we not there rewriting the drama, putting there what is not there, what is not intended to be there? Is the spectator really a significant concept in art? And what kind of art is that whose spectator owns its meaning? It will be easy to say that one can destroy the subject, be released of the ego and the personal will from the entire range of art; it will also be easy to say that one pretends this destruction or submission or guidance. At the same time, one might say that it is impossible to believe in any truly artistic production without being objective, without utter detachment of the self. An artist never grows tired of contemplating, even about the minutest fact. He never stops seeing like another man, another woman, another child, a god. For an art circumscribed by the unfree, cruel, and desolate culture cannot endure the time even when filled with eloquence. It will only be a block, with a peculiar shade, vulnerable to the lashes of stones and metal. Art's true goal is truth. Yet, it is the mind of the detached writer that does the work. How can artist be an artist if he does not say 'I' and run through the scales of his passion, desires, achievement, and failures, purging that disease of imagination? It might be possible. But as you think of classical tragedies, legendary tragedies, as I have chosen to call them, think also of the tragedy where you are destroyed. That's the perennial tragedy!

Do you believe?

"No!" the class chorused. They guffawed at the same time.

"Good! Let your mind do the work," he said and collected his book. Ephraim approached and carried his book as he usually did. A throng of students followed him.

"When are we going on a trip again?"

"Third Friday."

"Where shall we go, do you know yet?"

"To the theater."

"Theater!" they screamed.

"Yes. We shall see Soyinka's *Bacchae of Euripides*, and see how much he butchered his Greek sources or represented his anxieties."

Now, most of them disappeared, anticipating the journey to the theater. Some went into the restroom, some into the lounge to partake of their afternoon refreshment. Ephraim, however, followed Marcel to his office. He locked the door behind him.

"You were spectacular in the class today," Marcel commended him.

"I did my home work, that's all. If everybody had read the passages you gave us, they would not be so much awed," he replied, setting the books on his desk. He stroked his head very tenderly. Ephraim laughed and relinquished himself to him; it was a relinquishment in which he felt some bliss, the sort he had felt before over and over. Immediately, darkness stood around them with its own mind; then those ostensible eyes stood on his face and saw nothing but pleasure, plenty of it; the other pair withered as he was becoming numb with joy scourged out of his pain with immobile motion. Ephraim did not mind because he had come to *believe* that it was not strange.

# 3

Some months had gone now. Tracy had gotten very acquainted with the idea of marrying Maduka. She visited him, even more than she was welcomed.

"'Kem, I am going to get Tracy from the king's house," Anne told Nkem one evening. Troy was roasting yam in Elo's kitchen, blowing the fire with his mouth as he had seen Ifeoma doing. His head was ashy, his eyes bleeding with tears. His clothes were dirty, and his shoelaces were half burnt. On one corner, Elo and Ifeoma were sorting out palm kernels from a heap of chaff that they later made into a lantern. First, they took a long stick; second they piled the chaff around it like mud and set it under the sun to dry.

"Who wants some yam?" Troy shouted with a sense of victory carrying a bowl of yam.

"I do."

"I do."

He took the bowl to them.

"I shall run to the garden to pluck some pepper," he said and left in a little speed. Later, he came back with a handful of greenish and reddish pepper he ground and gave to Ifeoma.

"Take some to your father," Elo said.

"Okay," he said.

"Daddy, here are some roasted yam. I roasted them."

"You did what?" Nkem looked at the bowl of yam, steaming with freshness.

"Isn't it good, Dad?"

"It is, my son," Nkem replied, chewing a mouthful.

Meanwhile, Tracy and Maduka had come home. They went to different places; people still marveled at them and wondered why they were always together, being as young as they were. She paid them no mind, not even perturbed by the fury of their curiosity. She saw them as laughable, impoverished, and unkempt, even some of Marcel's students who threw about witticism that spanned through ancient literature. She sympathized with them, thinking that they were losing battle with life; yet, they knew more than she did, and spoke better than her. They were superb, vigorous, learned, and enviable. Her mood of freedom made it easy for her more than Maduka who always sought the cloud to cover him, to protect him from the eyes of the people. He was so disenchanted that the several chords which he could have pulled to get away remained in abeyance. Nonetheless, Tracy pulled him to herself; pride entered into her control; and the remainder of her manners followed sooth.

They were in Maduka's room, for his parents had gone away to a meeting. Maduka felt liberated. His masculinity took him over. He was in charge, and he ordered the servants regarding the chores in the house. Tracy plastered herself on Maduka; she lived for him; she played with him; she laid on him. Maduka detested that with acerbity, but that time, he pretended that he did like her laying on him. He covered her up with his body quivering with pleasure. But in all, that was the game where his desire for her persisted, even when smothered. He ran after her with jocosity, losing his shyness; then his virginity prevailed and wondered in his soul like a sentinel. They were overtaken by silence, which was filled with the murmurations of pleasure and enjoyment.

"Make love to me," Tracy slowly said.

"What?" Maduka replied and jittered. There was with it a sort of feeling of intimacy guided by the spirit of his childhood, his long saved innocence, the verisimilitude of his not being severe with and scornful of her. Simultaneously, he suffered throes of self-awareness; and there was something in him, which he denied, self-criticism, a coldness which he wanted to disappear; but it stood there and his body chilled with it.

"You are a chicken. Com' on," Tracy said

"Get out," he said and pushed her away. Accidentally, he hit her ankle on the stool. She cried. Maduka was filled with pity. His body shivered with compunction. He had never hurt somebody before. He looked at her crying. He was destroyed. He left the room. When he came back, she was still skulking. He pulled her up.

"I'm sorry," he said and held her. The holding turned into a hug, an embrace. His whole body assumed a new feeling, one that reminded him again of his virginity. He cleared his eyes and made her sit down again. Then she skulked a little further and stopped. She threw her head on his shoulder. Her hair circled around his mouth; pomade suffused him. Gently, he pushed her off and placed her head on his thighs. He bulged, nudging Tracy's cheek like a stone. Tracy knew and rubbed his legs devastatingly slowly. Fire kindled in his body. Tracy rose, overemphasizing the situation, kissed him.

"Make love to me now," she said slowly taking off her clothes. Maduka looked on with wide eyes. He became unconscious, almost hypnotized. He verified his nothingness; and it was filled with a tremendous substance, which surpassed his understanding and at the same time intoxicated him with the power of a narcotic. He fretted while she dragged him to the bed and laid down facing the ceiling. Her breast was shallow and unfocused.

"What is that?" Maduka screamed like one in a dream, pointing at her legs.

"What?"

"That."

"You are so innocent.

"No, that's not how it looks. That part needs to be cut off."

"Cut off?"

"Yes!"

"What do you mean, goddamn it? That's my body," she stood up.

"It is customary. You are not a woman yet with that."

"What?"

"Yes, it is the custom."

"Get outta here!" She slipped on her clothes. In a feat of anger, she left the room. Maduka followed her quietly wondering what he had done.

"Tracy!" Anne entered.

"Take me outta here. Now!"

"What's the matter?"

"I said take me outta here!"

"Tracy's mother," Maduka called while they drove off. They were engulfed in darkness in the car, a want of knowledge. They stared at themselves, seeing not their faces but their shiny eyes, which darted with perplexity, rancor, and opprobrium. They were together in the car, but Tracy was quite aloof. Anne felt annihilated; she begged to be accommodated; she yearned to be seen, putting her face forward, reaching out her hand, as though she is crying 'I am human.' In this very action tears consumed her eyes and flew on to her cheek, stream by stream. She was before her destroyer, fear and despair that had pulled the rope to the guillotine while laughing feverishly. She became burdened, now with misery, now with passivity, now with a conscious thought, which rose to a pathos. She began to die like a lily surrounded by fire and heat.

"What is it, honey?" She asked.

"It is this Mad—duka," Tracy began fretfully.

"What is it? Did he hit you?"

"Not just that."

"What else?"

"He said that my clitoris should have been cut off.

Silence over took them again. Anne was jittery. Her nerves became cold as her mind shot out in voyage of shame. But she blocked it, and neither did she explain to Tracy why Maduka said what he said. Altogether, she prized her daughter's fury and chastised Maduka in biting terms.

Maduka, himself, could not contain what he saw. He could not live a minute believing that Tracy was uncircumcised, which means that he could not marry her. What would his honor have been if he had not found out? He thought. He looked harassed, and he began skipping his meal, piling with sorrow because he had come to like her. Fever visited him. Then his parents began to wonder, because he had never been sick before. He swallowed to no avail several doses of paracetamol.

"Mama," he called one evening, still writhing with pain.

"What, Maduka?" her mother came.

"I cannot marry Tracy."

"Why? We have started planning the marriage."

"Stop planning, I cannot marry her."

"Are you afraid?"

"No, I am not."

"You like somebody else."

"No."

"What is it? Your father will be angry at you?"

"She is not a woman."

"She is not…? How do you know?"

"Do not hit me, Mama; she undressed before me."

"What?" She called the king who came in like an elephant. His voice was hoarse, bellowing like a trumpet. He looked at his son, then at his wife.

"What is it?" he asked.

"Maduka said that Tracy is not a woman."

"How do you know that," he said and moved to hit Maduka.

"Don't hit him."

"Tell me how you know."

"I shall tell you," his wife interceded.

"No, let him tell me since he is man enough to find out."

"I shall tell you," his wife continued.

"That's why you are sick. I cannot stay here and let my house fall down on me," he said and left with fury to invite the medicine man.

* * *

Anne and Tracy had just entered the house with a pretended decorum, peace and elegant. Tracy, however, was in her soul obliterated. He had never heard about circumcision. Her ignorance thus fired her agony. Quietly, she walked into her room. Likewise, Anne went into her room. It was getting a little dark. Troy was still in his dirty clothes, smelling with fumes and dust. Unlike Tracy, he was happy. Tracy had shut up herself in the room crying profusely, not understanding why Maduka approached her the way he did. She examined herself in the mirror; she did not find anything wrong with herself. She lay down, but she felt empty and alone, frustrated, and hysteric. She clasped her breast and sobbed, thinking of nothing but her body. Slowly, she looked between her legs; she wondered.

Looking for Troy, however, Ifeoma mistakenly entered the room. She saw Tracy looking at her naked body, examining between her legs. Tracy saw her and was startled. She ran, forgetting what her mission was, shouting 'mother.' She could not talk; all she did was pointing in the direction of the room.

"What is there?" Elo asked, pressuring her.

"Go there," she said.

Elo dragged her to the place and queried Nkem. Nkem denied knowing or seeing anything. Then Tracy came out of the room and pounced on Ifeoma who did not revenge.

"Beat her up," Elo screamed.

"No, no," Nkem interceded.

"She can't be coming into my room uninvited," Tracy explained.

"I thought Troy was there," Ifeoma said.

"Well, you thought wrong," Tracy added.

"Be nice, Tracy, she is your sister."

"No, she is not."

"But I did not do anything to you," Ifeoma said in tears.

Then, Anne came out. Elo had already dragged Ifeoma with her. Anne inquired about the cause of the altercation, shooting vituperation at Elo. Nkem paid her no mind, because he had made up his mind to live with their vaunted and whitewashed manners. Immediately, she took Tracy to her room; Tracy then asked her why Maduka said what he said. Filled with sorrow, Anne went through the whole story.

"Why wasn't I cut then?" Tracy entered in a paroxysm of emotion.

"I was saving you, honey."

"O! Saving."

"Tracy, a woman is a woman, anywhere, anytime. This barbarism cannot stop you from being a woman. Call it custom, that vaunted process of excising a part of the child, something that makes the child whole. There are all sorts of stories around it. It is said that at birth a boy possesses a female spirit around his genital, and a girl possesses a male spirit around hers. As such, these spirits ought to be cut off for them to be what they really are. When you were born, your father suggested that you be cut. I said no, because I was circumcised myself, because circumcision destroys women; I disagreed with your father because I stopped believing that circumcision has anything to do with a woman's femininity. Rather it destroys her."

Tracy became taciturn all of a sudden. Her mind was boggled. She began to notice some differences.

"Is it painful, Mom?"

"It is not just painful; it is murder. I cannot let you go through it. It is annihilation. There are things you feel as a woman which I don't."

Yet, there was fear in Tracy's soul, an impropriety, which she had come to realize, which she did not know how to approach. Sweat piled up on her face, as she ran around the market place with a group of young girls, and most of them were in Marcel's class. The most notorious one among them, Lucy, walked with hip gyration that was known to conquer all masculine sexual discipline; she possessed male magnetism. As they ran around, they wondered about what their parents had told them about circumcision. Lucy entered with utter certainty to deny all of them, maintaining that they are myths designed to uphold certain values. She even confessed that she was circumcised, and that nothing had changed about her. Tracy felt reassured and bid them goodbye. Then she struggled while she was held down, legs astride. Her muscle showed as she fought between two old women. Another old woman who had traded her teeth for nothing stood by, sharpening her knife against a stone. Her hair was long and dirty just like her fingernails. Her skin sagged considerably together with her breast that dangled like a balloon slowly losing air. She felt the edge of the knife. It was not sharp enough. She continued to sharpen it in silence and bizarre concentration.

"Stop screaming," Anne shouted at her and added her energy in holding her down.

"This should have been done long ago," Anne said again. Then, the old woman came slowly, for she could hardly walk having stooped so long while sharpening her knife. She sat down between Tracy's legs. She felt her vagina.

"My daughter," she said. "This is what you have been carrying. Women are not born; they are made like this," she said fumbling it; she touched a part which she pulled slowly and gently toward her body. Tracy screamed.

"Hold on, honey; it is over," Anne said.

Then she applied the knife with the dexterity of a surgeon. She did not look at what she cut. She flung it outside where chicken and hen battled for it. But blood oozed out. Tracy screamed terribly now. She rose in a pool of tears, examining herself.

"What?" Anne woke up too. Tracy was shivering; she could not talk; she sobbed and slowly gained her power of speech.

"I was dreaming. They cut it off. You were holding me down."

"Sleep, it is only a dream," Anne added.

# 4

The day came in seemingly slowly. It was cool; birds did not chirp so much. The sun was lost in the sky. A huge wind came; trees shook; ripe fruits fell en masse. The earth rose in piles of dust traveling here and there, meandering through the air, and blinding untrained eyes. The roads were swept on account of that. There was no one on the roads except Igbudu, a medicine man, who was answering a call by the king. He was also known as Anunuebe; also known as Iyi; also as Apiti; also as Ebini. Each of these names resulted from a medicine he made. Among them, people think Anunuebe was the worst. It was made mainly from Anunuebe, the magical tree. The medicine allowed him to disappear at the blink of his left eye, and was specially prepared to allow him to travel the spirit world—that journey earned him another name: *okara mmadu okara muo*—half-man-half-spirit. More like Gilgamesh. He saw no difference between night and day. And so people were afraid of him. His real name was Nwoke di Mma; like his other name, this one was symbolic. His father, who was also a medicine man, had difficult in getting a male child. His first three children were women. Because of that, the town believed the gods were punishing him for his evil deeds, but they were amazed when his youngest wife gave birth to a male child. In jubilation, he called him *Nwoke di mma*—a male child is good! Igbudu, however, was more diabolic with his medicine than his father; yet, he had not killed any man; and no man had attempted to kill him, for he had a considerable power to rob off people's happiness. He was not ugly, but he was not good looking either. All his hair had gone. His eyes were sharp like the eagle's.

When he arrived at the king's palace, he was in his porch. He was pale, as anger had overcome his face.

"His highness," he greeted.

"Igbudu."

"Why do you call me?"

"There's a snake in the rafter."

"Tell me in plain words."

"An uncircumcised woman came into my house. I was even planning for my son to marry her."

"Marry her? That's a taboo, your highness."

"Do you think I don't know that? I have just found out, and that's why I called you to undo whatever evil she must have brought with her ugly self to my house."

Igbudu looked on. He upturned his head to the sky. His face writhed. He shook his head and snapped his fingers time and time again.

"Does she know what it means? Does she have parents?"

"She was born in America."

"We are not Americans. Circumcision is our custom, does she know that?"

"I should think so; she is Maduka's grand-daughter. Yet America can do much damage to one's sense of self."

"Maduka! Hei! He will come and wring their neck. He never played with the custom of the land."

Next, he brought out his goatskin and dished his right hand in it for some dry leaves, which he crumpled and blew into the air, chanting some ominous song. Next, he brought some roots; he chewed them and spat them in four directions.

"No evil shall befall you. And your son shall not marry her," he said and waited, looking a little ghoulish, a little grotesque like a gargoyle.

"She has not brought any evil to your house, and she will not," Igbudu continued. The king became sorrowful, a sweet sorrow for he had disentangled himself from evil. But the thirst to have his son marry his friend's daughter was crippling. Its failure was like a taboo of its own.

"Our custom shall prevail," Igbudu said. But he hesitated in his heart, thinking wearily of what he had done. His soul ached.

Then, the king sent for his wife who came with a dish of kola nut. Immediately, she realized what had happened; sorrow overcame her soul. She suffered because she had lost a daughter in-law. Altogether, Maduka lost hope. But he was not devastated. His mother held him close often and kept suggesting the name of Ifeoma as a better woman. Maduka thought about Ifeoma and sulked, and dabbled to his defensive strategy against marriage, shrinking from a feeling that had more force. His mother reinforced her position by reminding her how marriage made men, and that if not, people would think that he was worthless.

At that time, though, it had spread through the town that the king had called off the marriage. People sniffed the air to find out the reason. They lamented because they had already sharpened their appetites; they felt it like a death. Nonetheless, they sympathized with Maduka and advised him to look the other way.

On the other hand, they detested Tracy, confirming their prediction: she was a worthless person.

"She has to leave the town."

"Yes, she must."

"What is it with circumcision? It is a normal thing."

"Of course, it is."

"That's what they learn from this white man country."

"Yes."

"Let's think otherwise, people. What happened to civilization?"

"Close your mouth, because you mean Western civilization."

"Yes, close your mouth, truth is truth."

Consequently, they tabooed Tracy. Nobody asked about her save Nkem and her mother, who suffered just like her. But she was undaunted, living as happy as she was strong; but in the house though, like a prisoner, without the sun or the sky. Tracy became taciturn, almost autistic, fighting, waiting to snap like a tight rope, waiting to collapse whatever was piled on her, waiting to die, to be absent, to be annihilated. But there was a life in her soul, filled with fire and energy, filled with hatred. She saw it herself spread over, heavy like concrete. There was no room for her to breathe. She was possessed by the desire to be free, but she was not herself. Her bosom rocked; her eyes turned gray; she grew taller.

Meanwhile Nkem and Anne did not talk to themselves. They bypassed each other like two pillars, elephantine. And between them stood unvoiced enmity, which contaminated the air around them. It was contagious and afflicted whoever came by, either by silence or boredom. Tracy was not perturbed.

One day Nkem was entertaining Marcel on the balcony. They were chatting about her situation.

"It is a shame that we've not learned, having come this far. We even refuse to learn. What has circumcision to do with what a woman is?" Marcel asked quite perturbed. Then Tracy saw that somebody thought otherwise and better than the hoi polloi. Nkem was silent. He looked merely, but he was calm. There was no madness on his face, then, not even in his spirit. He had become indifferent and cared very little about them. He looked around; Marcel was still there; he had broken out of the custom; he had reevaluated it and made it to fit his climate.

When Tracy came out, they were still there, but not talking too much. She was dressed. Soon, her mother followed, dressed.

"Where are you going?" Nkem asked

"I am out of this goddamned place. Eat your crudeness," Anne replied.

"Where to?"

"America."

"You belong here."

"No, you belong here. Come on Troy."

"No, I am not going. I am staying here," Troy said taking off his clothes.

"Please yourself."

They left for that haven where they will be appeased or applauded for their bawdiness, where no one will raise a voice at their taboos, where life *is* nothing but joy. Marcel looked at Nkem. All was silent.

# BOOK 3

# 1

2000. It was a season of anomie; or so it seemed, for life was brutish; hardship was a constant bedfellow for many, especially the poor and those who had no one in the high places or even someone who fed on the crumbs that fell from the tables of the almighty. Troy and his father, Nkem, were neither of these parties, and not because they lacked the unwritten particulars, for they were rich, and reeked of opulent idiosyncrasies, sumptuous food, clean houses, cold water, uninterrupted electricity, and more important, freedom and choice. Troy's father had chosen not to do anything with the rich; "they lack moral sense; at best, they are thieves and whore mongers," he believed and never hesitated to prove it. He vowed to instruct the people on the beauty of humanism and on the transitory nature of wealth and its adjunct peccadilloes. He never waned from tracing the anomie to the evils performed by the rich.

It was still morning then. The week had just started; Troy was on his way to school when he saw his father bemused before the television set.

"What's the matter? You appear agitated," Troy observed.

"The federal government just awarded twenty-five billion naira contract to Onye Ori Construction Company to rebuild a road that's not up to one mile and needs no renovation."

"Are you not used to that now?"

"No! I cannot get used to evil. No!"

Troy left him and went to school, understanding, however, his agitation. No sooner had he left than Ubeku, his father's friend, arrived with his usual pleasantries. He had retired from public service and lived at the mercy of benevolent spirits and his friend. Yet, he did not see himself as poor, perhaps, because he knew the white man's ways and had a command of English language; he often referred to it as "Queen's English" with impeccably enunciated "Q" and "E." He did not see himself as poor also because he had many children, seven; none of them was in the university then. His father had twelve, and he was the only one among them who reached standard six. The rest fell by the way and dabbled into several unsuccessful trades. They have joined the cadre of *le miserable* and urchins, who have been re-baptized by a few as the wretched of the earth, who were ever ready to assist in any labor.

"Ubeku! You are welcome. It's nice to see you,"

"You looked agitated, my friend."

"Agitated?"

'Well! Troy must have gone to school."

"Yes! A few minutes ago."

"You still insist you will not enroll him in the American International School?"

"What for? To join the elitist group? To be different?"

"I am just saying."

"Would you do that?"

"I am just saying that he should enjoy the benefit of his American citizenship."

"Listen to yourself! American citizenship in Nigeria! Have you heard the news today? Or should I ask you whether you have received your pension yet? The government which has not paid you awarded twenty-five billion naira contract to Onye Ori Construction Company."

Immediately, reality caught up with Ubeku, but it was already too late for him to understand or even deal with. He had already developed some kind of immunity to the frustration and some exits to the stress through animalistic and carnal engagement with his wife, whose wont it had been to obey, who always submitted with utmost respect, willy-nilly. That was how they got seven children. So, when Ubeku heard what his friend said, his body yawned for what had become his habit—to "shell" his stress in his wife's being.

"That's true," he said at last.

"True? Eh!" Nkem asked. "Do you still think of the American International School? I wonder! You may not have been any different from these goons of politicians if you had the opportunity. You don't seem to abhor their actions, but lament what you call your 'unfortunate situation.' Is there really providence in the fall of a sparrow or the shot of a distant and invisible hunter, or, perhaps, visible, but formidable?"

"I thought you would cherish the idea having studied in America."

"Not when the school is exclusive, reserved for numskulls because they have American passport and rich parents. Have you ever asked yourself how that institution came to exist here?"

"It's all for the better."

"Those students are not addressed as Nigerians; they do not enroll as Nigerians. What good is that?"

"Education," Ubeku was brief.

"No! They toy with our humanity. Especially when we subscribe to the principles and institutions that divide and disintegrate. All you need to create anomaly among a people is to tell them that they are different in manners," Nkem said and briskly walked to his room. Coming out, he brought the American International School catalog and shared the information with Ubeku. They saw that all of the instructors were expatriates; the curriculum was Eurocentric; even tuition was required in dollars.

"Is this the will of God, Ubeku?" Nkem asked.

Ubeku did not answer; he could not understand, for what he saw in the catalog was what he esteemed honorable and distinctive.

"Ubeku! Is this the will of God?" he asked again.

"No one knows," he replied suddenly.

"The will of God is essentially good—this is not!"

"I marvel at your position. I don't understand. You have American citizenship, the most coveted instrument in our country today."

"You don't know the stories, Ubeku."

"Tell me, then."

It was not long ago; people still remember how it happened. One certain doctor Okafor and his wife, a doctor too, saw that they had reached the apogee of the social strata, that no more transformation was necessary. They studied in America; they had American citizenship. I know them. Their children enrolled in the best schools. Now, they live at home because they have been assigned to the Ministry of Health. Their children did not follow them, of course. To ease the tedium of life, which was ever present in our country, to borrow a child, they went to their kinsman, Ndumbu, who was dying of poverty and suffering from multiple diseases. As was the custom among the poor in the village, he married late, and married a younger woman, Azuka.

They were seen as hopeless couple. Their marriage was scorned and was used as a symbol of doom, mainly because they did not have a son. Their two female children, Nneka and Ego, were seen as expendable and as instrument of nuptial negotiation or system of transfer of right and continuum dependency. Azuka who was far more aware of the culture blamed herself and incessantly pressured Ndumbu to marry another woman. He paid her no mind, for he believed nothing was wrong with their situation, even though their parents have stopped visiting them. Yet, in the privacy of their minds lurked the wish of their daughter-in-law's pregnancy and a male child. Who will inherit your wealth? They always asked. They punctuated their world with the desire of this dream child.

As Christmas approached, the dream intensified a propos the birth of Jesus Christ. The air changed; roads were no longer famished; all roads led to the village, and Azuka who usually left for the village early in December refused to do so this time. Ndumbu could not make her go; he dabbled into his memory; he remembered his parents' words. Next, he saw a dancing group with his parent exhibiting unutterable joy, brandishing their ornamented hands in the air to the tune of the traditional music. They embraced Azuka, who was dressed in a maiden's beauty, and showered her with gifts and chorus of prayers. 'The gods shall bless you with many children, boys and girls.' 'You shall see your children's children.' Immediately, he heaved a heavy sigh and resigned.

"Okafor, God will bless you abundantly. Take Nneka as your daughter, and she will call you father and your wife mother."

Ndumbu turned to Nneka and advised her accordingly. Simultaneously, his wife was shedding tears of both joy and sorrow. For she could not stand giving her child away; yet, she could not offer her what she needed to grow into a woman.

That's how Nneka came to live with Okafor, exchanged with the hope of charity and the belief that something good goes with those who lived in America. But no sooner had he arrived than Mrs. Okafor absconded from the kitchen and all chores she was very familiar with. Nneka cooked, cleaned, scrubbed, washed, and ironed all clothes. Mysteriously, she did that with good heart. She believed that she was doing what she was brought there to do. Dr. Okafor did his part as well; he sent money to her parents.

As time went on, Nneka grew. She became voluptuous. Mrs. Okafor did not see that because Nneka was doing her work religiously, but Dr. Okafor did, and took advantage of that several times. He realized that she had been cut; her clitoris and labia were excised; what he saw was a small orifice; he understood what he saw; he was used to it, so, he did not hesitate with his journeys that were accompanied initially by Nneka's silent screams of pain. On subsequent journeys, the scream was displaced by silent moans of joy. So, Nneka blamed the pain on her virginity. As they said, she became more beautiful day by day, and she began to recognize her beauty and Dr. Okafor's surreptitious dependence on her for carnal currency; she could not resist, and she did not know if she wanted to or not; she was just a slave, a servant, whose desire was mainly to serve her master. Then, she started avoiding some of her duties, and to Mrs. Okafor's petulant anger. She blamed that on her ravishing beauty and self-consciousness; she believed, in other words, she had stopped doing her work because she, Mrs. Okafor, had cleaned her up. Suddenly she saw herself in Nneka, her beauty and growing elegance; she could not understand because Nneka was poor, and was doomed to be poor; more so because she believed there was a connection between the one's intellect and social status, so elegance was reserved for the rich.

"Why didn't you wash all the dirty clothes," Mrs. Okafor asked her.

"I became a bit tired and stopped, Madam. I will surely finish it," she replied.

"Will finish it? You will finish it now," she added and slapped her with unutterable velocity. Nneka was perplexed, not because of the pain, but because she had never been slapped before.

"What did I do, Madam" she asked, sobbing profusely.

"You wretch!" she hit her the second time and ordered her to finish the work.

That's how the abuse continued, or the euphemism they used to describe such treatment, discipline. Mrs. Okafor affirmed her difference vehemently by beating her in the name of correction. Dr. Okafor did not pursue the incidents because he had scarred her with a worse wound. To cut the story short, Nneka ran out of their house—to their amazement—and went home. Yet, no one in the village heard about anything, except about Nneka's ingratitude and poverty. Her father said nothing too to avoid the proverbial blame.

"I have not heard that story. The gods of the poor is ever awake," Ubeku added afterwards.

"That's another dimension of the postcolonial. And you will never hear it as long as you worship these American citizens here. You see, Nigeria is just a haven for taboos as America. They know that."

They continued their conversation; Ubeku had begun to fidget in his mind, not knowing whether to believe his friend or to assert his original belief. Then, Troy came in, a little famished.

"Good afternoon, Sir," he greeted Ubeku.

"My son! Welcome!"

"Welcome!" His father added.

"How are you father?" Troy asked.

His father looked at him and nodded in affirmation. Troy concurred.

# 2

2020. A nameless time. Nkem rose with the crow of the cocks as he did ages ago, and passed both his right and left palms across his face—one after the other—to ward off some sleep in his eyes. He dusted his chest, which was dotted with cilia rather than hair, brownish and fragile like his whole frame, where bone and flesh are now indistinguishable. At best he walked crooked, with each step accompanied by a seemingly excruciating pain and a guttural moaning. He grabbed his walking stick, shaking like a lily in the proximity of a tornado; yet his grip was firm.

"Troy," he called in asphyxiated tone.

"Papa," you called. "Good morning."

"Morning, my son," he replied. "I am tired of calling you Troy, I have to find you a native name" he added with petulance discharged with both hatred and concern. Troy smiled, for he did not care so much about the name himself; he was stuck with it since his mother chose it.

"Why are you smiling?" his father asked. "Have I said something foolish?"

"No, Papa! I cannot allow myself such latitude."

"What bears your smile, then?"

"The thought of name change."

"Oh yes! Troy does not tell me anything about you, except that you were born in America."

"It has its own meaning, though, Papa."

"Meaning? Tell me."

"Do you know Homer?"

"My son! Book wisdom will destroy you. When the intellect grows without the spirit, knowledge is still not born. What has Homer to do with you?"

Troy did not answer; he sat down, for he realized that his father had begun one of his homilies and exegetic revelations. Troy thought of Helen of Troy, of the Trojan horse, and began to explain the symbolic nature of his name—symbolism his mother did not think of. He saw himself as a hidden truth, a truth only time and circumstance will reveal. He thought of his mother who left him and his father at their village because she was inebriated by the American fashions and the facile ways of life that came along with utter and irrational license; he thought of his mother who did not witness his daily conquest in the village with animal traps and masquerades.

He remembered vividly when and how she left, that's after a disagreement with his father because his sister, Tracy, was not circumcised, and as a result lost her suitor.

"My son," his father began. Troy was startled.

"You are not in America, but America is still in you. Homer does not have the universal principle. Do we have to go to the West before we can appreciate ourselves? We lose ourselves in that venture."

"Papa, why do you say so?"

"Who among the natives who has gone to America do you see without blemish? Who among the children do you see act differently from them. I always think I am in America here. Let us go to the market place and you will see for yourself."

They left their house that morning; they did not care about locking their doors; they trekked. The sun has risen in the azure sky; birds had already begun their daily routine, as sheep bleated in their pasture. Market women, carrying their livelihood on their heads thronged the roads. Some were young; others old, and of different sizes—some with extensive and corpulent posteriors; some with pendulous and loose breast; some skinny beyond imagination, with scars of wretchedness etched on the heels of their feet. Their movement exuded blues as their wrapper forced their way through the air and aided by the flip-flap of their slippers and the havoc of their feet on the road. They shared distant and familiar stories.

"The old man is going to the market today," one of them called Enuma observed. Leaving her basket on her head, she pointed at the old man.

"He is with his son," another joined.

The younger women among them did not have any opinion, for what they knew of them were only narratives. Enuma prevailed though; she was a paragon of gossip.

"I have heard so much about these people," Enuma continued.

"What have you heard, you, word don't pass you."

"His son was born in America, and his daughter was not circumcised."

"I heard that, too."

"His wife left him because she did not like our way of life, even though she came from the next village. She wants to do everything her own way like American woman."

"What else did you hear?"

As Enuma thought of an answer to that question, they all walked close to the old man. Exchanging greetings, they passed them by, stealing a glance at them, perhaps, to verify whether what Enuma had heard was true; to see the traces of America, or the decay that was America.

"Good market to you all," the old man said.

"Thank sir," they said in unison.

"Good market to you, too," Troy added.

"Thank you, my son. It shall be well with you," they replied moving faster.

The market was already teeming with a huge crowd; it was a curious sight; the crowd remained the same with throng of people that were pendulous, a complexity of people—dark, pale, white. A pin will not find its way to the ground; it was a beautiful hullabaloo, an ecumenism of voices, distinct merely as an infinite shouting. Buses, motorcycles dropped and picked passengers, and consistently beside a mechanic workshop, which was known as a symbol of infinitely deferred dream, and mainly because of the mechanic himself, Etolue. The workshop was his Cambridge, the subtle salvation of his mind. He was noted to have challenged his Mathematics teacher with some formula unknown to the teacher; yet poverty robbed him all chances of further education. He was not the only one in that group. Around his university were elderly men, who passed time towing cups of palm wine down their throat. They shared impeccable English and with erudition, and assumed knowledge of distant ideas, yet they had only attended the village schools.

With all theses noises, the old man inched in; he exchanged

glances with them, but none of the glances from them registered the old man's humanity

"Here he comes," one of them said. "You remember him? Maduka's son."

"Efuluefu! Good for nothing man. The story goes that he did not circumcise her daughter, and he is hiding her in America."

"It is the market day," another said with sarcasm.

"Yes. It is; as kite perch, so will the eagle. Is that not what our ancestors said?"

"So it is."

The old man arrived and took a seat on the pavement close to the elders. He was older; they appeared like young men beside him.

"Greetings," he almost bellowed at them. The elders mumbled their responses. He immediately recognized their disposition in that suffocated and suffocating greeting. He smiled, though, and directed Troy to a handful of people in the crowd to demonstrate his argument that America flows in the blood, that America is no longer a place, but a sensibility, consciousness that could be enabling and corrosive at the same time.

"Do you see that man, the one in white T-shirt and jeans, with a basket?" the old man asked Troy.

"Yes, I see. What about him?"

"Do you see any other man with a basket buying food and with a child? Look over there? Do you see men killing cows? Over there men buying and sharing palm wine? Do you see anyone with a child and a basket?"

"No. And...?"

"That man has been to American, and he is still there."

As they deliberated on the consciousness of this man with a

basket and a child, a throng of boys and girls in their teen jumped out of a car in an unfamiliar excitement. No one in the market wondered about them, for they are used to them already. The only dark skinned one among them had a wavy hair; the rest bordered on low and high yellow. Their facial features formed a tapestry of human civilization and traversed Europe, Asia, Inca, Hispaniola, India. No one noticed them. They did not understand them.

The boys had on bandanas and sagging pants; the girls had tank-tops that showed the excesses of their succulent breast and jogging shots that wrapped their buttocks in a seductive grip. The market was all the mall they could get there.

"Hi y'all! Let's check out the ice cream joint."

"Word! It's crazy hot."

"It's my treat this time."

"Cool! If you are down."

"Have you watched them kill a cow?"

"Das gross. I've seen it."

"Not really! It is fun, like, like, you know. They tie the legs, like, like you tie a rope, and the cow will like, like, like fall. Next, they drive a sharp knife through its neck like that. It's tight."

"Check this out! I heard they collect the blood and eat it."

"No shit!"

"Yeah! My dad did that once and made pepper soup. It was the bomb, y'all."

"You are something. Let's get ice cream."

"You better get used to it."

They flocked around the ice cream shop that had served only a trickle of customers at that time. They called for most exotic flavors.

At this juncture, the old man uttered, "that is exactly what I mean. What civilization is that? Listen, you can hear their names. Tamika! Shawn! Pedro, Aida."

"Names! Civilization! Are they not human beings?"

"*Mmadu*? Human beings? That is not enough. You need a root. Without that, you are nothing," the old man said.

"Papa, you agonize over nothing. These are the liminal children of the new world."

"Book wisdom," the old man said. "You mean *usu*? That's what we abhor. It is in our adage, the bird of the night."

Troy smiled in his usual way and quite unperturbed.

Feeling he had made his point, the old man rose and started walking in his snail speed home, thinking of a native name to give Troy. None came readily. None even stood out in his mind.

# Epilogue

Now, whatever may lie at the bottom of my story, whatever you may have seen in it, let it be a question of the first rank; let it be a personal question, one laying bare your beliefs, and not one querying the beliefs of the other person you don't know. Stories are spiritual things. They have dual power of hiding and betraying a consciousness. It is art, and should be treated and taken as such, even if it longs for the ugly, the stout will of pessimism, the tragic. It is free. But how I regret that I do not have the courage to destroy this story, not to tell it. It might be my death to have told it, my destruction; but I have chosen to die for my story. Lift up your heart and listen to it! I have put on myself the crown of your laughter: I am potent for it. I beseech you, laugh. Imagine a generation scared to tell its story or scared to tell the story of another which leaves a sour taste in the mouth with its unfathomable decrees? What is it? Whatever may lie at the bottom of my story, it is a task to prepare you for what is yet to come, a moment of self-consciousness, when a mind shall gaze both forward and backward and pose the question of 'why and wherefore' of its culture, its destruction and dilution. My story concludes with a separation, which is the necessary option of things that cannot be together. Listen, I am not in the best of health now. I am fatigued. The sky is cloudy and the wind is getting cold. It might rain exceptionally heavy tonight. Sleep might be impossible on account of it. I'm invaded by it already. Let us disperse now for another day. Let us save our gestures, our accent, our denials for the benediction of the story. Farewell!

Printed in the United States
56705LVS00002B/223-279